That Magic Touch

Triplets: Three Aren't One

Book Three

by

Dani Haviland

USA Today Bestselling Author

Copyright

Book Description

Brought up in the backwoods by a father dedicated to helping those less fortunate, Ria was a genius at healing but ignorant of life and relationships. Would Evan be the one to show her what made life bright and enjoyable?

Praise and Awards

USA Today Bestselling Author

Kindle Top 100 Bestselling Author

Amazon Top 100 Historical fiction Author

Amazon Top 100 Biographies and Memoirs Author

Amazon Top 100 Short Story Anthologies and Collections

Amazon Top 100 History of Women in the American Civil War

Amazon Top 100 United States Drama and Plays

Amazon Top 100 LGBT Mysteries Author

Amazon Top 100 Weddings

Amazon Top 100 Satire

"There wasn't a heartstring this one didn't pull at! And, no spoilers, but that's one of the nicest endings I could have imagined – all round, proving redemption's possible, some things will last forever, and …. Karma. This isn't just a story of Jose and Loren; it's so much more.   Amazon reader on *Too Fast for You* (http://bit.ly/2fast4YOU)

"From the picturesque descriptions of the Alaskan wilderness, to weaving a beautiful love story, the author's writing style is both serious and quirky. A perfect, relaxing read!"   Amazon review of *One Arctic Summer* (http://bit.ly/2OneArcticSummer)

Dedication

This story is dedicated to Diana Gabaldon. A long time ago, she shared that if writing is what you want to do, do it! Write, write, write! I did and have found that just the thought of creating people, intense situations, and surprising solutions brings a smile to my face. Whether your passion is reading, writing, singing, teaching, healing or the arts, readers, follow it. Just don't forget to share the wisdom of following your dream with others.

Chapter 1: Previously

January 3, 1992

Gloria leaned forward, steadying herself on her husband's arm as she stood on tiptoes, trying for a better look. "Is that them?"

Roger gave his wife's hand a reassuring pat, then moved away from the group to check out the station wagon pulling up to the gas pumps. "I don't know. Did he tell you what he'd be driving?"

"Oh, yeah. He said he'd be driving a white van," she said. "Remember the password: Woodstock."

"Sounds like my kind of guy," Luther, the other father-in-waiting, remarked. He hugged his wife around the shoulders. "Remember when we were there?"

"How could I forget," Leanne giggled. "Over twenty years ago, and now our baby is finally here. That's a long gestation!"

"There he is! There's Chuck!" Gloria exclaimed, hopping up and down with joy at seeing her new friend driving into the convenience store parking lot.

"Settle down," Roger said. "You don't want to bring attention to us."

"Two middle-aged couples, snuggled up against the wind, looking like vultures ready to pounce… I'd say we were already suspicious," Luther said.

"Conspicuous," Leanne whispered.

"Whatever," Luther said with a shrug.

Chuck, driving the new-to-him white van conversion, looked beyond the gas pumps and saw the two couples standing by the bundled firewood, their smiles of anticipation marking them as the new parents. He waved briefly as he rolled past, coming to a stop near the alley at the end of the building. He felt safer in the dark, out of sight of everything but owls searching for dinner. "Tranquility base: Stork One and Stork Two have landed," Chuck said to his female cohort.

The neo-natal nurse, snuggled up to the gym bag full of newborn baby girls on top of the foldout bed behind him, grunted that she'd heard him, but didn't comment.

A mixture of fear and excitement washed over Chuck as he got out and approached the huddled foursome of wannabe parents. "Anyone for a game of golf? Is there a good course around here?"

"How about Woodstock?" Gloria said, then ran up to Chuck and gave him a big hug. "Are the babies inside? Are they okay? I thought I was going to have a total meltdown when Dr. Buddy called and said the mother had died, and that they couldn't get the babies out in time. Chuck, he said that Grace and all three babies had passed."

Chuck's eyes widened. "Grace was alive when I left." He opened the side door, exposing his new traveling nursemaid and the bundle of babies.

"I'm still alive," Grace Two said indignantly, then groaned softly as she realized it was a misunderstanding about the name she shared with the babies' birth mother. "I think you'd better call me Nanny." She looked at the eager parents crowded around the open door, the women squeezed in front of their husbands to keep away from the chill. "Why don't you ladies come inside?"

Gloria led the way, Leanne right behind her. The younger of the two peered into the unzipped bag. "Which one is ours?"

"It's between you two who gets Aqua and who gets Pinkie. The yellow-wrapped sweetheart is mine," Chuck said, watching the allocation of babies from the front seat.

"Oh, my God!" the silver-haired Leanne exclaimed. "They're identical! I can't believe it. How will we know whose is whose?"

Little Pinkie opened her eyes, started to squall, then caught sight of Gloria and smiled. "I don't care if she's the biggest or not; this one's mine."

"Then that must mean she's ours. Oh, I can't believe it. I swear I feel a tingling in my breasts. I'm as barren as a moon rock, but I swear she's kicked in a bucket load of estrogen." Leanne looked up. "Can I take her home now?"

"That's the plan," the nurse said. "Oh, and don't even try to get in touch with Dr. Buddy. Either of you. If they haven't caught him yet, they will. You're lucky Chuck and I got in the middle of this or you wouldn't be celebrating motherhood tonight."

"Thank you," Gloria said to the nurse. "Truly. Chuck has my number. If you two run into any trouble or need a few bucks, just give me a call." She unzipped her jacket and put the swaddled baby inside. "Come on Vickie. You're coming home."

Leanne copied Gloria's tactic of coat kangaroo-pouching her baby. "And you, too, Tori Lynn. Daddy's waiting outside."

Leanne stepped out of the van, then suddenly yipped. "She latched on! Oh, my Lord! I'm going to see if Luther can set me up with some of those plant estrogens. I may be able to nurse my baby still! Sing hallelujah!"

***

"That went well," Chuck said after the two couples had left. "Are you ready to hit the road, Nanny? Hmm. I really do like that name. It fits you. No nonsense, but nurturing."

Grace Two, now renamed Nanny, couldn't help but smile. "New name, new beginning. Works for me. Did you remember to pick up distilled water for mixing the formula? I didn't see any in here."

"Oh, shoot! I'm glad you noticed. No, I forgot. I'll run in and get some right now. Do you want a soda or coffee or anything?"

"Coffee, black, would be great."

"I'll get you something else, too. Stress eats up calories and we have a long way to go," Chuck said, then mumbled under his breath, "Wherever it is we're heading."

Chuck walked in the convenience store and looked around. "Where do you keep the water?" he asked the clerk.

3

"What is this? There's a real run on bottled water tonight. Back there. See that kid with the ball cap? Yeah, right next to him."

"Thanks. And is the coffee fresh?"

"Just made a pot. Don't tell me; you want a giant chocolate bar, too," the clerk said, adding a chuckle.

"Hey, that does sound good."

"Just follow the kid. He's after the same stuff."

Chuck went to the back of the store where the young man was and found the water. "Dang!" he said, checking the label, then noticed the kid had picked out a bottle with a different colored cap. "You got the last distilled water, didn't you?"

Dusty lifted up his jug of water. "Shoot. I don't want this kind. Here, I'll swap you. I was after spring water for drinking."

"Thanks," Chuck said, then headed to the coffee kiosk. "What did we do before convenience store coffees?" he commented.

"Shoot. I don't know," Dusty answered. "I don't think I was born yet. For me, they've always been around. I didn't even know what a rotary phone was until I was clearing out my dad's attic. I can't imagine having to stay in one room while talking, tethered to a six-foot curly cord."

Chuck blew out a breath, stopping short of a full laugh, and shook his head. "Yeah, our folks really had to rough it. Have a good night, what's left of it," he said and saluted the young man in farewell.

"Yeah, you, too," Dusty said. "I know it's going to get better because I just found my woman. Thank you, Lord!"

Chuck paid for the water, coffee, and candy then walked to the side of the building and rapped on the side door of the van. "What's the name of Snoopy's bird?" he asked.

Click.

The young nurse opened the door and let him in. "Do we have to keep doing that?" she asked.

"No, probably not. I'm just trying to bring a little levity to this harrowing evening. I know my emotions are all over the place.

4

Elation at getting out of there with all three babies alive; fear of either being caught by Buddy's crew or being charged as an accomplice by the FBI; excitement with being able to help two couples get the daughters they were told were dead; and absolute sadness and loss at having to walk away from Grace. Lord, I hope the guys got her. Oh, shit!" he said, his voice loud as if he'd just been pinched. "I can text them!"

Chuck pulled his cellphone out of his front pocket and tap, tap, tapped the quick message to his father. 'Did U get her?'

***

Dusty handed the jug of water and chocolate milk to Hal, his girlfriend's father. He may have just lost their twins in a tragic birth, but at least he still had her. And a great support network of family who cared for her.

Beep! Beep!

"What was that?" Dusty asked, looking around.

"My cellphone," Papa Doc said. "I got what they call a personalized alert tone for my incoming texts." Chuck's father took the blocky gray cellphone out of his shirt pocket, tapped a few buttons, and then put it back in his pocket. "Someone just checking to make sure all went well on our end," nodding to Grace.

"It's going to take time for my daughter – hell, all of us – to heal," Hal said. "Some losses take longer to get over. Let's hope you haven't lost Chuck because of all of this."

"Only for a little time. My son has a nurturing soul and is a gentleman. I think he's just stepping back so Dusty can help her heal."

"What do you mean? He didn't know Dusty was coming with us or that we even found him," Hal said. "That was last minute, remember?"

"Yeah, I wouldn't know your son if I sat on him," Dusty said. "Hey, does anyone want some chocolate?"

Grace listened to the men banter back and forth, their voices rising and lowering with their emotions and concerns. She hadn't

5

heard her father and two surrogate uncles in a month and didn't realize until now how much she had missed them. She looked out the window. The world was getting better, itty bit by itty bit. Dusty was here. Would he accept her as she was? The way he had held her – sobbing uncontrollably with joy – when he rescued her after she had been abandoned by Nurse Ellen, she knew he'd do anything for her. He seemed to be sharing her feeling of loss for the babies, too. All her men could mourn with her. And they would heal together, too.

All but Chuck. Where was he? She closed her eyes tight and tried to find a thread of recent memory, struggling to recall the last words he had said to her. There it was. An echo of his words. He was leaving her, he said – leaving so she wouldn't associate him with her loss.

Which would have been worse, the loss of the babies to adoption or death? Definitely death. With adoption, they would still have been happy little people with families who cared for and cherished them. Now with death, they were just little corpses. Was it her fault they had died? Did she do something wrong?

Grace looked at Dusty, blinking back the tears that had returned. A familiar movement out of the corner of her eye caught her attention. She leaned over him to watch the man coming out of the convenience store. "Who's that?" she asked, pointing out the window.

Dusty recognized him as the man he had swapped jugs of water with. "Just some guy from the store. He got coffee and water, too. Why? Do you know him?"

She sighed then leaned back into his arm. "I thought I did…"

"Grace, I know it's not exactly romantic – my timing and all – but I want to make a new life with you as my wife. I have a lot going on now. I have my own business and everything. I still want to marry you and always will. We can start again with a family as soon as you say the word. I kinda know what went on with the other guy, and it doesn't matter to me. I mean, I know you have been hurt in about a million different ways, but I want to help you heal. Would you let me? I mean, I'd do it however you want, but I'd rather do it as your husband than as your best friend."

Grace leaned into Dusty and inhaled his unique scent of boy and man. She felt the first smile in ages come to her face. She looked up. "Yeah, I think I'd like you better as a husband. Let me get healed up, and then let's get married. But if you don't mind, I'd still like to live with Papa Doc and Silas for a while. And hang out with my dad, too."

"And me?"

"Duh! You'd be living with us, too. One great big dysfunctional family."

Chapter 2: His Girl Friday

Rrrr. Rrrr. Click. Click.

"Crap!" Chuck groaned. He smacked the steering wheel in frustration, then looked back at the stunned nurse, holding the baby close, bouncing her gently to settle her down.

Little mews of discontent seemed to be working up to a full roar. "This isn't going to work," she said. "This baby's hungry. Come back and feed your daughter."

"But the water's cold. Won't that upset her stomach?"

"Just get back here and I'll see what I can do about the engine," she said indignantly, shifting toward the end of the bed, making room for him.

Chuck made his way between the front two seats into the back, then flicked on the overhead light so he could see. Nothing.

"Just what I thought," his frustrated cohort said. "Here, I took a few bottles of the pre-mixed formula from the clinic before we left. I stuffed one down my bra so it'd stay warm. I suggest you do the same."

"Huh?" Chuck asked, shuffling around her so he could sit down.

"Not stuffed down your bra, doofus!" she said. "If you always keep one stashed next to your chest or belly, it'll be at body temperature, ready to feed her when she's hungry."

Tingles of anticipation and appreciation ran up Chuck's arms and down his shoulders into his gut, settling into a warm glow of nurturing comfort. His daughter. He sat down and snuggled the child close. Yes, she was his. Rockets couldn't blast her away from him now. Nor could a piece of paper. Grace may have known about the first two, but this third one – this bonus baby – had been his spirit child since the day he first heard her heartbeat.

The nurse's hand bumped his, offering him the bottle in the dim glow of the convenience store parking lot. "Helluva a way to start life, eh? Let me go see what I can find out," she said, then scooted out the door.

Scores of times over the past eight months he had tried to talk Grace into keeping the babies. He'd spent hours trying to convince her that with all of the loving people she had in her life, they would certainly be able to keep her 'twins' out of reach of her evil mother. Would she have willingly given him the third child if she had known about her? Since she had already refused to keep the first two, it really didn't make a difference.

"Quit beating yourself up, Chuck," he said softly as he fed his baby her first meal. "You presented every possible argument for her to keep them so many times, it pissed her off. Her fears could not be abated by logic or tempered by hope, no matter how much you tried. Twice she signed papers giving them up. She was one determined woman."

He should feel bad that she had been left with nothing, but that wasn't the way it was. She was left with a loving father and two surrogate uncles who'd reshape the world for her, one of them his own father. Plus, Dusty, the man she had sacrificed it all for – saving him from her mother's vendetta – just might come back into her life now. Maybe she'd catch up to him after her body had healed. She could share or withhold the information about losing 'twins.' That was her decision. Only he and a very limited few others knew that she – Grace Stillwater – had birthed triplets. This little gem was his. Rhianna Lynn Armstrong. The shadow. The echo behind her sisters' heartbeats.

The side door opened. "Got any tools around here?" the former neo-natal nurse now acting as mechanic asked.

"Yeah, some came with it when I bought it. They're stashed under the passenger seat in a box."

That door shut and the front one opened, bringing the temperature of the conversion van down to near outside temperature: below freezing. Chuck unzipped his coat and snuggled his daughter close, one hand next to her cheek keeping the nipple in her eager mouth. "There, there, Ria. Daddy has you."

Is this a sign of things to come? Everything falling apart around us? Am I being punished? By doing something I thought was right – giving these three girls families who could not have children any other way – was I playing God? Did I make Him angry? Lord, I did what I thought was right. Yes, it was a bit selfish to take one of them for me, but I really felt as if she was meant to be mine. Really. Truly.

Vroom!

Chuck was startled out of his introspection and prayer of contrition by the sound of the engine roaring to life. The hood closed with a clunk, then his female companion opened the door and put the toolbox away. She looked back and saw his wide-eyed, slack-jawed expression. "What? I can do more than stuff a bottle in a baby's mouth or wipe her ass. I have skills. Now, what direction are we going? I think I'll take the first shift. Looks to me like you have your hands full."

"South," Chuck said. "But can you drive a manual transmission?"

"Give me a break. I can fix 'em, drive 'em, or steal 'em if I have to. I've been on the streets since I was just a bit bigger than your little nugget there."

"Okay. Oh, and just for the record, I think Nanny is a poor choice for a new name for you. You're more of a Friday."

"Friday. I like that much better," she said. She settled into the driver's seat and buckled up. "Come on, Miss Daisy. We're headed south, leaving the ice and snow to the crazy Yankees."

***

Three days later

"How far south did you want to go, Chuck?"

"Until it doesn't freeze at night or we run out of money," he said. He rubbed his sleep-deprived eyes. "Where are we now?"

"Florida. Would you believe they have a Woodstock here, too?"

"I'm beginning to think every state has one. Just like every town has a Main Street. Do you feel like splurging on restaurant food? I'm getting tired of canned food and crackers."

"As long as you're buying. I only managed to get a few bucks together. I pretty much was a slave to Dr. Buddy and his outfit. I don't like to think of myself as a thief. I was just taking what I thought I earned. I'll never get back what I deserved, though."

Chuck rubbed his hand over his face, confused and disoriented. "I don't think I'll ever be able to make up to you what you've meant to me, and it's only been a day or two since we met. I can start with pancakes and real coffee, though."

"It's been three days, Chuck. You're sleep-deprived. You have mommy brain. Watch out that you don't get the baby blues, too."

"Huh?"

"Let's eat," she said. "Mom and Pop Pancake House sounds like a winner to me. Look there: 'Try our bottomless cup of coffee.'"

"Yeah, too bad you can't buy a good night's sleep as easily."

"Since you don't have a final destination picked out, how about we get something to eat, and then find a wide spot off the side of some back road to park for a few days? You need to get caught up on rest before I leave."

"Leave? Friday, where and how are you going?" Chuck asked, his voice pitched high in panic. He groaned softly as he realized how desperate he sounded. "I'm sorry, but I really didn't know that taking care of an infant was going to be so labor-intensive. How in the heck am I going to see patients and take care of a newborn at the same time? And wherever you're going, do you think they'll need an on-call doctor? Could we work together for a while? All I need is enough for food, gas, and formula."

"I don't know where I'm going, so I guess to keep you from losing it completely, I can stick around for a while. At least until Little Bit gets on a schedule."

"She's already on one. One ounce of formula every hour. It takes fifteen minutes to get that in her, and then she's out again. How do mothers do this?"

"Most mothers' babies are bigger than four pounds. Her

tummy's too small to hold much but she still digests it at the same rate. Her feeding intervals will get longer as she grows. And most mothers either nurse the baby and or they have a partner to help take care of it. I really don't have a destination, so I'll hang around until I do, I suppose. Come on. Run a comb through your hair and throw on a clean shirt. I'm hungry and I swear I can smell that coffee from the parking lot."

"Well, I know I can smell the bacon," Chuck said, hastily taking off his shirt. He rummaged through his backpack, coming up short, then felt a nudge. "Wear this. It's mine but doesn't look girlie."

"Thanks," he said and pulled it on over his head. "Nothing girlie about you, Friday." He looked up and noticed her scowl. "And that's a compliment, not an insult. Just in case I offended you…which I didn't mean to."

"Yup, you're sleep-deprived, malnourished, in need of coffee and could use a partner, Mr. Mom."

"I agree to all but the last one. A girl Friday will work just fine for me. You're not the kind of *partner* for me in that respect."

"Good to hear," Friday said, setting Ria in the car seat-carrier. "Hand me that little receiving blanket. I'm going to tent the car seat. It may not be cold here, but I don't want restaurant germs settling on her. And make sure you wash your hands before touching her after we leave. She doesn't have an immune system yet."

"How about you go in without me and I'll stay here with her?" Chuck asked. "You have me scared now. Just order something to go for me. How about bacon, pancakes, and coffee?"

"Nope. You're coming in with me. You're not going to become a germophobic hermit, trying to keep your child from experiencing life. Yes, she's not getting anything out of this excursion, but you need it. Remember, if you're going to have a mobile clinic, you're going to need to learn the area. Listen to conversations, ask about local medical care, pop in at the library and do some research on their computers about median income and family size. Find those areas where there aren't any services."

"Maybe you're right about needing a partner. I may have the medical skills, but it seems like you have the social and promotional talents required to find my niche."

"Niches. We don't want to settle into one area for too long. At least, as long as I'm with you. I'm breaking my own rules committing to hanging out with you two for more than a week or two."

"So, you'll stay?" Chuck asked, hoping he didn't sound like he was begging.

"As long as you don't piss me off too much, fuzz face. You're either going to have to buy a razor or grow a beard. You look like a homeless druggy."

Chuck stepped into the front of the van and pulled the rearview mirror down. "Jeez! Why didn't you say something?"

"I just did. Don't worry about it. When we go in with the baby, they'll know you're the dad. You look more like a new father than an addict."

"I guess it's going to get better. At least, I know not all parents look this rough."

"Wouldn't know for sure. I never had one around long enough to find out."

He glanced sideways at her, not wanting to address the remark but wanting to see her reaction to sharing a small part of her past. Yes, she regretted it. She was looking away, her lips pulled tight in a scowl. "Let me get my wallet. I'm buying," he said, wondering if it was her child or parent who wasn't around long enough. Or both.

Chuck popped open the dash and looked for his wallet, noticing something that wasn't there before. He didn't unwrap the red handkerchief but nudged it with the side of his hand as he grabbed the billfold. A gun. Yes, she was being cautious. Very cautious. He would need to be, too.

***

"Well, that was extremely satisfying on two levels," Chuck said, bounding into the back of the van, Ria still asleep.

13

"I take it you're still cool with me driving?" Friday asked.

"Hey, you heard the directions just as clearly as I did. I never took you for the chauffeur-type, but I'm notorious at getting lost."

"I'm going to fuel up, pop into the store, and grab more distilled water. Do you want to take a nap in the parking lot? Ria seems to sleep better in the car seat than even snuggled up to you. You'll get better rest if she's not right next to you, waking you up with every little movement."

"Yeah, let's give that a shot. That is if you don't mind."

"Would you stop saying that?" Friday said, a low guttural growl escaping. "You sound so needy."

Chuck laughed. "I am needy. But thanks for telling me. If we're going to get along, we have to be honest with each other."

"I agree. That being said, while I'm in the store and before you fall asleep, would you use some of those baby wipes and give yourself a sponge bath? You're getting ripe."

"Okay... I guess a once a week visit to a truck stop would be in order."

"Huh?" Friday asked.

"They have public showers. You know, pay to suds and rinse."

"So do lots of laundromats. I'll ask around about that while I'm in the store. Wash up, then go to sleep. She isn't going to stay zonked out for much longer."

Chuck yawned. "Don't have to tell me twice," he said, then pulled a blanket under his chin. His neck slumped to the side, and he was out.

"Sweet dreams, Dad."

After getting fuel, Friday pulled over to the less-traveled side of the store which was also closer to the pawn shop. She reached in the glove box, took out the handgun she had taken from the clinic and shoved the bandana-wrapped package inside her flannel shirt. She closed the van door behind her. "Thanks for helping Chuck start his clinic."

Friday walked out of the pawn shop with a mere four-hundred

dollars, a lot less than what she thought the ivory-handled pistol would fetch but a lot more than his initial offering of one-hundred. It wasn't until she took it back, ready to walk out of the store, did he slip and let the gun lust sparkle in his eyes. It wasn't the most valuable handgun around, but it was unique. No receipt requested also helped the transaction. Yes, the gun was going underground and would never be recovered by Dr. Buddy. She snorted as she pushed the bills deeper into her jeans pocket. Back to where it had come from.

***

Tap. Tap.

Chuck looked up from giving Ria her bottle to the rapping on the window. He started to get up to open the door but was stilled by a familiar voice.

"I got this," said Friday. "I just wanted to make sure I didn't catch you in the middle of your bath."

The back door opened and a whoosh of cold air entered the van. Chuck brought the blanket up around Ria. "What'd you get besides water?"

"Not now. Let me unload so I can shut the door. I have a full tank of gas, but I don't want to burn it up running the heater if I don't have to."

"Ria's fed and should fall asleep as soon as we're moving again, so do you want me to drive this time?"

"Nope. I asked around when I was shopping. I think I've found our destination. I'll drive until we get there. If there's an available spot to stay for more than a night, you can unload and set us up." Friday climbed in the driver's seat and cranked up the ignition. "Then I'll get some sleep."

Ria and Chuck slept for the next three hours until the van stopped. The crunch of gravel roused the dozing father, a smile spread wide. *I don't know how long I slept but I feel great!*

Tap. Tap.

Chuck pulled back the curtain, verified it was Friday, then

15

stepped out and looked around. "So this is it?"

"Looks decent enough to me. There's a campground down the trail, outhouses are walking distance and downwind, and there's a creek that's supposed to be full of fish. Oh, and lots of folks living rough who could use a healing hand."

"Sounds like this crazy man's Eden," Chuck said. "Give me a sec and I'll be out."

Verifying Ria was still sleeping, Chuck grabbed the white and red cotton baby-carrier sling he had bought on his shopping trip with Gloria weeks ago. After a few adjustments for his larger-than-a-typical woman's size, he slipped Ria into it. "Ah, my little *bambina*, all ready for Papa to work."

The refreshed new father, having enjoyed another nap, reached his arms out and around to check his range of motion with the baby cradled next to his body.

"Looks like you're pregnant," Friday said with a chuckle.

"That's the first time I've heard you laugh," Chuck said, finishing his stretch.

"First time anything's been funny in the last four days," she replied coldly.

"Ouch. Too true," he replied with a grin of irony rather than respond with her same snarkiness. He opened the back door of the van to reveal her generous load of supplies. "So, boss lady, what do you need for me to do here?"

"The rest of the stuff can be dealt with later but for now, how about setting these tarps up? I got some rope and bungees, too. I figure you needed one to keep the rain out and a few others to keep the privacy factor up for your patients. Oh, and the camp chairs are for us to share with them as needed." Friday reached into her back pocket, pulled out a packet, and tossed it to him.

"What's this for?" he asked, checking out the multipurpose knife, still in its original packaging. "And did you steal it?"

"It's a Leatherman. Other than a hatchet which is already in the tool kit under the front seat, it's all you should need out here. And I spent enough money at their store that I figured they shouldn't mind that I gave myself a thank you gift."

"Yeah, speaking of that, where'd you get the money for all this? I still have my cash on me."

"I got skills," Friday said. "And since it's been almost two days since I've had any sleep, I'm taking my break. Set this place up as you'd want it. Just a hint, though. People might not like being seen approaching. Leave a subtle entrance from the back for the bashful folks who don't want others to know they need help."

"One outdoor clinic with public and discretionary accesses, coming up." Chuck nodded to the side door. "The bed's all yours. Sweet dreams, and once again, thanks."

"Yeah, well thank you, too. I needed a way out of that nightmare. I only hope that they did catch up with Dr. Buddy. Someone has to shut down guys like that. He's hurting too many people on both ends. Taking babies from the girls by claiming to help childless couples – which would be all right if he'd let them go back to their old lives and families afterward, not kidnapping them and keeping them as birthing vessels. And the new parents – taking their money, getting them all worked up with a baby on the way then telling them the baby died. He's making himself rich and breaking hearts all over the place in the process. Sorry. I'm tired and rambling. If you find something you can't handle, leave it until I wake up on my own. I'm going to bed."

Chuck brought up his hand to give her a reassuring pat on the back that he had it handled, then realized she wasn't the touchy-feely compassionate person he was and would take offense. "Night-night."

Readjusting his daughter in the sling so she was out of the way, Chuck pulled out all the supplies he thought he'd need and the camp chairs. "Come on, darling. You're going to help Daddy build his first mobile clinic. How about calling it 'Doc's Clinic'? Do you like the sound of that?"

Ria's hand reached out then settled under her chin, a sweet

smile on her face, her eyelids fluttering as she dreamt. "What do babies dream about?" he asked softly. "Well, I hope they're happy thoughts and hopes. I know mine are. And they all settle around you."

An hour into his set up, Chuck came to a point where he couldn't progress without a second set of hands. "Sorry, darling. Your little hands aren't strong enough to help yet. But they will be one day. You just sleep and grow for now." He set up the red camp chair and kicked out his legs, visualizing how he could make this work. "One of these days, we'll have a real motorhome with office space and an exam room and even a kitchen and bathroom with running water. How am I going to potty train you on a five-gallon bucket?"

"Need a hand there?" a friendly male voice called out.

Startled, Chuck sat up quickly, instinctively covering Ria from any potential harm. He stood up and turned to face a tall and handsome man, broad-shouldered and with a grin that could melt the heart of any man or woman. "Oh, hi. Yes, as a matter of fact, I could use an extra pair of hands, if you don't mind."

"Looks like your arm's broke and you don't care to use your sling. I know I don't."

"This?" Chuck asked. He held out the edge of Ria's sling and glanced into it to make sure she was still sleeping, a smile broadening his face. "Oh, this isn't for a broken arm. Come here and look."

The whiskered man in his thirties approached, looking side to side to make sure this wasn't an ambush. A squirrel ran across the ground behind him and up the tree, startling him. He looked down as he walked, back in defensive mode, searching for IEDs. The ground was cleared. He was safe. No insurgents.

Chuck noticed the signs of PTSD. The man was probably one of the people 'living rough' that Friday had mentioned. The noises and pace of city life weren't comfortable for many who had it. Post-Traumatic Stress Disorder wasn't necessarily treatable but he knew

18

not to make any sudden movements.

"Oh, my goodness!" the man said in a hushed whisper. "That's the smallest baby I ever saw! Is it yours?"

"One hundred percent mine," Chuck said.

"And your wife?" the man asked, suddenly glum. "What does she say when you say that?"

Tentatively putting his hand on the other man's shoulder, Chuck looked him in the eye and said, "Don't have one. Never did. She's adopted by me alone."

"Oh," the man said.

The sparkle in the man's eyes let Chuck know that he was interested in him in more than just a 'setting up camp' way. Playing house together might come in later!

"Oh, where are my manners?" the man said, his hand thrust out to shake Chuck's. "I'm Harvey. This area has been my home for…for a while." He shrugged a shoulder in embarrassment.

Chuck took the strong hand in his, unconsciously sighing at the touch of another man who might be willing to be more than friends, then realized they had been holding hands a little too long and let go. "Oh, and I'm Chuck. Here's what I have to work with," he said, pointing to the opened tarps strung through with ropes. "I'm trying to build an enclosed structure. I'd like two entrances. You know, so folks won't see who's coming and going?"

"Ooh. You're building a privacy shelter so you can play doctor. Sounds like fun to me," Harvey said, eyebrows raised suggestively.

Chuck blushed and Ria squirmed at the same time, his sudden warmth disturbing her rest. He leaned forward just a bit to let air get between their bodies, then waited while she settled back to sleep. "First things first: privacy. And yes, I will be playing doctor, but I really am one. This is my mobile clinic."

"Not too mobile if you're attached to a couple of trees."

"Hey, it's a starting point. Rome wasn't built in a day and all that. I had a clinic in a building in the past, but life changed. I'd rather bring up my daughter in fresh air and sunshine than smog and

19

fluorescents."

"So that's a girl?" Harvey asked, nodding to the sling.

"Yup. So," Chuck said, changing the subject. "If we get this done before she wakes up, we might have a little time for a cup of coffee. At least, I'm pretty sure I have some left."

Harvey brought his arm up around Chuck's shoulder and gave him an affectionate squeeze. He bent close to his ear and whisper, "Coffee not required."

Chuck blushed again but moved Ria away from his body before she got too hot. "Then let's get on it!"

"Words I thought I'd never hear again," Harvey drolled, then picked up the tarp half-hanging from the tree. "Hold this here and I'll secure it. I can put this up by myself, but I'm rather enjoying the company."

"Me, too," Chuck said. "Me, too."

Twenty minutes into their set up, Ria awoke. No slow announcement of her hunger this time, she went from sound asleep to squawling within two seconds.

"Oops. 'Scuse me for a few minutes here," Chuck said, sitting down in the camp chair. He pulled out the warmed bottle of formula from his tee-shirt pocket under the sling, stuck the nipple in his mouth and quickly licked any lint from it, then offered her the bottle.

Harvey picked up the other camp chair and set it up across from Chuck. He leaned forward to watch, his jaw dropped open in awe. "Wow. A guy can do that?"

"I hope so because that's my plan," Chuck said, leaning back in the chair, his legs kicked out.

Harvey sat back and copied Chuck's pose, bringing his boots up next to his, playfully rubbing them back and forth.

"Bootsies?" Chuck asked.

"Huh?"

"Well, I've heard of playing footsies, but bootsies?"

"Feed your daughter and let's see what else we can come up

20

with, all right?"

"Oh, very all right," Chuck sighed, his boot rubbing Harvey's.

"What's going on out here?" Friday's voice boomed.

Startled, Harvey tumbled out of his chair and rolled to the ground, coming up in a crouch in a fighting position, the knife he pulled from his belt held at the ready.

Chuck pulled his legs back and sat up as straight as he could in the saggy-bottomed cloth chair, trying to regain composure.

Ria screamed at the sudden tension in the air, letting everyone know she needed to be seen to first.

"Well?" Friday echoed, lifting her chin at the stranger in her camp. "Who are you and why are you here?"

"Damn it, Friday!" Chuck said. He stood up awkwardly, using both hands to hold Ria close. He bounced her gently and tried to calm her. "This is a public clinic. Or will be. You have to get used to strangers coming in."

"You said you didn't have a wife," Harvey said. "So, does this mean she's *just* your girlfriend?"

"Hell, no!" Friday and Chuck said at the same time.

Friday glared at Chuck at his reply even though she had given the same one. "I'm his assistant," Friday said. She inhaled deeply as she realized that these were just two guys wanting some alone time together. How would she feel if he had intruded on some hoped-for intimacy for herself the same way?

"Sorry," she said, genuinely humbled, her hand out in greeting. "We've all been a little short on sleep for the past few days. If you two are okay, give me the baby. I'll see if I can settle her down inside the van with me."

Harvey stood up and quickly sheathed the knife. "Friday?" he asked, shaking her hand firmly, looking deep into her eyes.

She returned the greeting with the same brisk social posturing. "It's not the name I was born with, but I answer to it."

"Fair enough. I'm Harvey. No one uses last names around this place. So," he nodded to Chuck, "he tells me he's a doctor. What's your story?"

"I just work with the guy. Broken people come to us and we patch them up as best as we can with what we have."

"Nobody 'round here has any money," Harvey said, his eyes narrowed as he looked at the two of them as if they were con artists.

"Did you hear her say anything about fees?" Chuck asked. "I only charge what a person feels my time is worth or what they can afford. I accept all forms of payment. As far as I'm concerned, you just paid in advance by helping me out. Do you need anything fixed?"

Harvey snorted in derision. "You saw the way I jump at sudden noises. I don't think you have anything that'll fix that."

"Nothing I sell or can get my hands on," Chuck said. "If you would, spread the word around the area. I don't have much to start with, but I do want to help others. I've got skills and training. People get sick or injured and have pains. I just want to make people feel better. That's it. Plain and simple like me."

"Well, there's nothing plain and simple with lofty goals like that, Chuck." Harvey reached out and shook Chuck's hand in farewell, his hand settling on top of Chuck's for an extra moment. "I'll see you around." He opened up the pleat in the red and white sling and looked down at the sleeping baby. "She sure is pretty. Congratulations, Dad."

And then he was gone, silent in his trek through the forest floor, an expert at being quiet, quick at disappearing into the trees.

Friday and Chuck watched the silent exodus until Harvey was out of sight. Ria lay content, snuggled in Daddy's warmth, her fist in front of her mouth, comforted by its nearness.

Friday finally spoke up. "It looks good," she said. She pulled on the tarp and saw it could easily be pulled open, riding on the roped-laced eyelets like a shower curtain on a rod. "Nice touch. Come on. Give me a hand with organizing what I picked up at the store. You're the one who needs to know what we have on hand and where it is."

The two worked together for twenty minutes, combining the scant supplies Chuck had already purchased with the ones Friday had just picked up. "Where'd you get the money?" he asked again.

"I got skills," she replied, using the same answer.

"I know that. I just want to make sure you're not stealing folks blind and I'm going to get in trouble for it. Or even worse, lose you."

"You don't need me," Friday said.

"I need you a hell of a lot more than you need me! Ria and I both need you. You may not like the idea of family, but if we're going to live together, we're family. And family needs to be honest with each other."

"Okay. I stole a gun from Dr. Buddy's office. It was a fancy one with ivory handles and gold inlays. I took it to the pawnshop in the shopping center and got four-hundred bucks for it. I managed to stash a few bucks in the lining of my gym bag over the years but keeping us poor is one way he kept us on hand. I want to keep that as my seed money."

"You're not very old. Are you a registered nurse?"

"Nope. Ellen taught me what Dr. Buddy wanted me to know about babies. Neither one of them wanted me to know more than what I needed for pregnancies, deliveries, and neonatal care. If I had a degree, I would have found a way out earlier. So, yes. I want to learn everything you can teach me while I'm here."

"No problem," Chuck said. "But that won't help you on the outside. I mean, the real outside -- the legitimate world – not off the grid, working in campgrounds and parks."

"We'll see where life takes me. Who knows? A few years down the road, maybe I'll break off and start my own rural clinic."

"I'll see if I can find some medical books at the local libraries while we're on our healing mission. I don't plan on staying anywhere for too long, though."

"I'd ask you why, but I really don't care. Your reason is yours alone. Not mine."

"No," he replied, setting his hand on top of hers for emphasis. "My reason is mine *and* my daughter's."

Chapter 3: Adjustment Period

Six months later

"Did you know it was going to get this hot?" Chuck asked.

Friday chuckled as she twisted up the bottom of her tank top and pushed it into her cleavage, creating a sort of bra. "It is summer in the south, you know." She took a long pull from her water glass. "Damn! I wish folks would pay you for work with ice cream instead of ratty blankets and wilted veggies. I'm sick of soup and we have enough blankets to make a mattress!"

"Even ice cubes would be appreciated. I did get some beer from one old guy. Do you know how bad it tastes warm?"

"Got any left?" Friday asked, head tilted, a sly grin growing.

"Five out of a six-pack, why?"

She reached out for it. "Because I can stash it in my secret spot. That's where I haul the spring water from. Creek water is tainted most of the time, but I found where it bubbles out of the ground, cold and clear…"

"Grab the kid and a bottle, and I'll put up the closed sign," Chuck said. "And bring that map. Let's go research our next location. It has to be somewhere higher, though. I wasn't cut out for the heat. At least, without an air conditioner."

"Pussy!" Friday said, laughing with abandon.

"Meow," Chuck replied.

The three hiked up the hill to an overgrown area, so verdant that it seemed to create a mountain out of the vines and brambles. "Here," Friday said.

Chuck took the long branch she offered him and turned it over in his hands, noticing it was well-worn from being handled. He looked at her, eyebrow raised. "And…"

"Your arms are longer than mine. No matter how far I reach, I always seem to get scratched. Since you're about a foot taller than I am, your reach should be a lot longer, too." She took back the stick for a moment and inserted it into the brambles. "Right here. Pull

25

back with the crook end and discover my little heaven on earth."

Friday took the baby and carrier off Chuck and slipped it over her shoulder. She bent forward and held Ria close while Chuck held back the thorny branches and twisty vines, providing a prickle-free passage for them.

"Wow! Why didn't you tell me about this? Good grief, this place has to be at least ten degrees cooler than our campsite."

"If we both were hiking up here on a regular basis, folks might get the wrong idea," she said. Chuck answered her with a scowl. "All right, all right. The truth. I've never had anything of my own. I was the youngest of eight kids and got everyone else's hand-me-downs. It wouldn't have been so bad except the next three oldest were boys. I never even had a second or third-hand dress until I was ten, and that was because a neighbor lady felt sorry for me. It was at least a generation out of date, but I felt so pretty, twirling around, the skirt spinning out away from me..."

"You know, you really are a pretty woman, Friday," he said, not looking at her, instead marveling at the little pool fed by the spring. He squatted down and gently set the cans of beer in it.

"Yeah, a whole hell of a lot of good that did me in life. When I got knocked up, my parents sent me away, and then I had the baby literally torn away from my arms. I know she was alive when they took her. She was only sleeping. I know it!" she hissed, trying not to scream and upset Ria but finally letting it out after all these years.

"Did you look for her?" Chuck asked.

"How could I? I had nowhere to go. I was healthy, young, and gullible. They could pretty much do whatever they wanted with me."

"So, you were locked up?"

"More or less. They kept me around to help the other girls who were pregnant. They offered me good money. 'What else are you going to do? Become a hooker? We'll give you a decent wage plus room and board to help the other young women here. But if you don't want that, go ahead. You'll be scorned. You're already a fallen woman to your family.' They messed with my mind, Chuck! I was a child. Shit, in some ways I still am. I'm only twenty-two!"

"Well, if it makes you feel better, only your frown makes you look older. When you were laughing a few minutes ago, you looked like a teenager. Free from the cares of the world."

"But I'm not free. I'm trapped again. No skills, no family I can talk to or go back to. We're two paupers, trying to help others, out on some sort of fantasy quest. Shit, we don't even have enough money to pack up and go somewhere where people pay real dollars for your skills. You'll be working for scraps and someone to haul firewood for the rest of your life if we hang out here. We – rather, you – need to find an angel who'll fund you at least enough for a halfway decent motorhome. Something with running water and a solid roof, not a tarp and water hauled from a spring or creek in gallon jugs."

"We'll leave here and I'll find the money. Mark my words, we'll go pack up camp and leave at the crack of dawn. However, for right now, I'm willing to see if this beer is cooler than warm." He picked up one out of the chilly water and handed it to her. "Cheers?" he asked.

She took it and saluted him with it. "Okay, but one thing…"

"Hmm?" he asked tipping back the brew. "Ah, close enough to cool. What else do you want?"

"I want that third beer. Equal partners in the goods we take, at least the stuff worth a darn."

"Sounds good to me because, hey, if you weren't here, I wouldn't be able to do much more than see one or two people a day. Babies really are labor-intensive."

"So I'm just finding out." Friday grabbed a beer and popped the top. "Maybe one of these days, I'll get to find out for myself," she said and tried to gulp away the start of another bout of depression. "Maybe."

***

An hour later – all the beers and the baby's bottle finished –

Chuck held Ria over his shoulder, trying to urge a burp out of her. "Well, are you ready to head back, Friday? And since we've both had a few, make sure we don't forget to get more bottles fixed for my little angel."

Friday gently touched Ria's cheek. "You know, it's a good thing she's fair and not dark-haired like my little girl. I would have run like the wind with her the first time your back was turned."

Chuck's mouth gaped in shock, then quickly shut as he realized it was the beer talking. Maybe. "Well, as you've found out, being a single parent isn't easy. Even though I've never heard you say it, I'm sure you love her. Maybe not as much as me..."

"Chuck, the more I get to know you, the more I like you. I'd pretty much given up on..." Friday opened both hands and looked around. "Given up on everything. Then I see the love and devotion you have to your ideal and your little family. I guess all I need is my own ideal and family."

Reaching out with his free arm, Chuck gave Friday a quick hug. "You *are* family. Our family."

Friday looked up into Chuck's bright blue eyes and swooned. She hadn't had a man since she was five months pregnant with the baby she'd lost. Even then, it was rough and without pleasure. There had to be more to sex than grunting and sharing body fluids. Surely, Chuck would be a gentle lover, one who saw that she was satisfied before he achieved completion. She closed her eyes, puckering up as she imagined gentle caresses and kisses...

Chuck pulled back, releasing Friday from the hug, turning away from her lips that were suddenly a mere inch from his. "The sooner we head out, the quicker we'll be done with breaking camp. We need to catch a few hours of sleep before leaving. Daylight comes pretty early in the summer. Actually," he babbled, standing up awkwardly and grabbing the grotto-entry stick, "our business at this site has pretty much come to a standstill. I think folks come by just because they're bored and want someone to talk to."

A slight groan escaped Friday as she realized she had just hit on

Chuck. Yes, he was physically appealing and probably the nicest man she'd ever met. Scratch that – he was the nicest *person* she'd ever met. Why did he have to be gay? "Sorry," she mumbled as she moved past him while he held the briars and vines back.

"Hey," he said softly, coming close to her. "It could have just as easily been me except I think I have more tolerance for beer. We're both in need of someone. Let's hope our next site has more to keep us busy and focused."

"And maybe an available guy for both of us," she added with a nervous chuckle.

"I'll second that one," Chuck said, following her as she led the way down the slope.

A few minutes later, they arrived at camp and saw a client waiting. Or at least a person kicked back in the red camp chair.

"Where you been?" Harvey asked with a tinge of jealousy. He looked Friday up and down, his eyes narrowed, then smiled flirtatiously at Chuck.

"I should ask the same about you," Chuck said, his hand reached out in greeting. "I haven't seen you in months. Actually, since the day we met."

"Oh, I had to leave to take care of some stuff. I was just wondering if your little friend there could watch your daughter for a while. Maybe you could come up to my place for a drink or two. You know, spend some man-to-man time together," adding a wink.

Chuck felt his loins tingle and his gut knot. He'd just promised Friday he'd tear down their site tonight so they could bug out at dawn. It wouldn't be right to ask her to do it all the work plus watch Ria. Especially since it was just so he could get laid!

"Dang," Chuck groaned and shook his head. "I'm going to have to say no for tonight. Actually, probably forever. We're leaving and we don't even know where."

Harvey's chest puffed up in indignation, the tattoos on his lower arms twitching as his muscles flexed. "What? You just come back from getting a little with your baby mama tart and don't want a little of this?" he asked, grinding his hips seductively.

Friday's eyes widened at the bulge in the man's pants. Everything about him was physically perfect but his package was so huge, it was practically obscene!

Chuck saw how red Harvey's face was getting and turned toward Friday. He slipped out from under the baby's sling, offering it to her with a nod that said, 'Watch her and take care of yourself. This might get bad.'

"I've made a commitment," Chuck said calmly once his ladies had left the area, "and I intend to stick to it. As far as what goes on between Friday and me, that's our business. Now, if you didn't come here to have me see to a medical condition, I'll have to ask you to leave."

"You owe me!" Harvey growled. He reached out and yanked on the rope that secured one side of the strung-up tarp, pulling it to the ground. "I helped you set this place up, so you owe me!"

"Well, it looks like you're undoing what you did, so I'll consider that a wash."

"Why you pantywaist little cock…"

Chuck threw a short blow just below Harvey's left ribcage, dropping the big man to his knees with the quick but efficient hit. "Please leave now. And as far as the kidney injury goes, there's nothing I can do for it. Only time and rest will mend it. Get out of here and never darken my life again."

Harvey stumbled to his feet, clutching his side, a dribble of saliva hanging from the corner of his mouth. "It's not over, Doc."

"Actually," Chuck said, "it is."

An unintentional groan escaped Harvey as he moved to get up. He struggled to stand up straight but made it. He took his first step forward, then stumbled as the pain overwhelmed him. One hand shot out, stopping him from biting dirt as he fell down. He tried to resume his cock-of-the-walk strut that had worked so well in prison, then relinquished himself to the fact that he'd have to stay hunched over to move. "It's not over," he repeated softly, then shuffled into the brush, branches breaking, his mumbled cuss words eventually fading into nothingness.

"Wow! That was intense," Friday said, coming out from behind the van once she was sure Harvey was gone.

"How's Ria?" Chuck asked. He looked close to search her face for signs of being traumatized, then up at Friday. "And how are you?"

"She's fine. I'm scared shitless," Friday admitted. "How's your hand?"

Chuck turned it over and looked, then brought it up to his lips to check for small contusions or ligament tears that weren't yet visible. "Hurts like I smashed it into a rock. I guess knowing the human body's weak spots comes in handy. That and being a Golden Gloves boxer when I was a teenager. I about killed one older brother with a blow like that. Not literally, but it did keep him off my back for quite a while."

"So, what do we do first? Soak your hand in a little Epsom salts solution?"

"Yeah, you're a quick learner. Here, I'll take Ria if you'd be so kind as to set me up."

Friday slipped out of the sling and transferred it to Chuck. "Think of it this way. If we weren't already leaving, having a goon like him after you would be a good reason to get out of Dodge. He's spooky."

"Yeah, we have our guardian angels looking over us today, that's for sure."

***

The next morning was chilly and clear and full of promise. "Wake up, Sunshine," Chuck said, nudging her with a cup of instant coffee.

Friday groaned, started to roll back over, then popped up, frantic. "Is he here? Did Harvey come back?"

"No. Relax. We're loaded up and ready to go. Here's some coffee to get you started. We'll splurge on bacon and egg breakfast

31

sandwiches and a fast-food bathroom washup."

"You're so generous," she said, taking the cup from him. "Give me a few and I'll be ready to pilot or co-pilot; your choice."

"No, it's you who's so generous, Friday. I hope you stick around a lot longer. You really are family."

***

The next day, further on down the road

"Good news," Chuck said, handing Friday a cup of convenience store coffee.

"You mean other than not having instant coffee for breakfast?" she asked.

"Yup. While I was paying for gas and getting Ria's water, I met a guy who asked if this was my van conversion. Seems like he has a motorhome that's too big for him and his wife, and he'd like to downsize. We're going to meet him at his place and do some straight across trading. I hope."

"If it has running water and a roof that doesn't leak, I'm all in."

"I didn't say the same thing, but I sure thought it hard enough. I don't want to play hardball, but if we can get a little cash or something else we can use, I'll see if I can work that into the deal. Oh, and when I saw he was wearing a cross, I sort of lied…"

Friday scowled. "You mean, you lied. There is no such thing as 'sort of lied.'"

Chuck rolled his eyes. "I told him we were married and Ria was our daughter. She's fair like I am, so it's not a big stretch. How about we were married two years ago? January third sounds good."

"Ria's birthday. And where are we from?"

Chuck downshifted and pulled up in front of a large home overloaded with aging trees. "Everywhere, I guess. We'll have to wing it. We're here."

"Wait!" Friday said, reaching out to stop him. "Don't you think we might want to use another last name in case Harvey's still on the prowl?"

"You're right. Let's drop the first part, just in case he's smart enough to tail us. That's the other reason I want to swap vehicles. I don't think he'll be looking for us in this older middle-class neighborhood. It doesn't fit my job description."

"Mrs. Chuck Strong," Friday said, then brought up her bare left hand. "I must have lost my wedding ring."

"Or we used it to trade in for this. A little sympathy may go a long way. Just in case, would you see if you could tidy up a little while I'm inside talking?"

"Yas-suh, master," Friday said in a deep southern accent. "Anythin' you say, boss."

"Grr," Chuck growled, then opened the door, reaching back to pat her on the shoulder. "Thanks."

"Go, go! Before he changes his mind!"

Five minutes later, Chuck and the RV owner were back. "Mr. Baker, this is my reason for getting up each day...unless the baby gets me up first. My girl Friday and the woman who makes me smile, Grace."

Friday was all smiles at the clever introduction, but her face fell momentarily when Chuck used the name she had used at Dr. Buddy's. She quickly regained her composure and smiled, reaching out to shake his hand. "Nice meeting you, sir."

"Oh, just call me Pastor. Everyone else in town does. So, do you mind if I look around?"

"No problem." Friday picked up Ria and the car seat carrier, handed it all to Chuck, then got out. "How about we wait under the tree?" she asked.

Chuck looked back and forth, then sighed. Hopefully, Friday had put the magnetic sign with his real name on it under the mattress or some other out of sight place. The last thing he needed was to lose the deal because he had given a false name.

"Did you tell him you were a doctor?" Friday whispered to Chuck as she settled down next to him on a grassy spot in the shade.

"No, why?"

"Duh! You have pharmaceutical drugs in there!"

"Shit!"

"Yeah, shit. Go explain," she said, shooing him away. Friday looked back down at Ria, now wide awake and reaching for her. She took her out of the carrier. "Come here, Little Bit. Daddy's going to get us a bigger home, one with running water and room enough for you to crawl in. No? You don't want to crawl? You want to go right from rolling over to walking?"

"She's adorable," a voice from above them said.

"Huh?" Friday looked up and saw an older woman, probably the pastor's wife. "Oh, yes, she is. I'm Friday. Well, Chuck refers to me as his gal Friday."

"You two been on the road long?" she asked.

"Ever since Ria was born," Friday answered with a shrug, glad she didn't have to lie.

"Yes, Pastor and I were traveling ministers. We'd go from one hardship area to the next, ministering to the poor and needy. Then the church would send us down the road again. We had our first son in a little van just about like yours until he was two. When I was ready to have my daughter, we told the church board that we really needed bigger accommodations. They had us set up over in West Virginia just after Mary Catherine was born. She only lived with us in that little thing for two months."

"And then you got a bigger home?" Friday asked.

"Nope. She caught pneumonia and died. Pastor put his foot down after that. He said I'm not sacrificing any more of my children. Either get me a solid roof and indoor plumbing or I'm changing affiliations. Well, they got us this big house and we've been doing the Lord's work in this area ever since."

Friday's hand was on Mrs. Baker's at the word died and stayed there until she finished her story. "Do you want to hold Ria?" she asked.

She nodded and sat down next to them. "You're so lucky. I never got to see my daughter get this big. This one's tiny but she seems to have great motor coordination. How old is she?"

"Six months," Friday said, handing her over. "She was a month early."

The pastor walked up to the trio. "Looks like you have a babysitter at the ready, Mrs. Strong, if you want to come and check out our old motorized Conestoga."

Friday smiled at the man as he spoke, but couldn't help flinching at the name Mrs. Strong. "Please, call me Friday," she said. "It's not the name I was born with but is the one I'm comfortable with."

"Amen to that. The Lord works in mysterious ways," the Pastor's wife said. "Catherine never felt right. You can call me Kitty."

"Yes, Kitty. She's already fed and should be dry. If not, let me know and I'll take care of it."

"Oh, I know my way around diapers. I even have a few in the house. We have a closet full of goodies if you're running short." Kitty double-checked the snugness of Ria's onesie tee-shirt, too small to be buttoned at the bottom, and saw it was a cloth diaper on her, not disposable. "On second thought, you go ahead and check out the ride with the men. Little One and I are going shopping."

"Oh, no…" Friday started, not wanting to be obligated.

"Nope. Let an old lady play dress up for the daughter she never got a chance to raise. Whether you trade or not, the clothes are yours to keep."

"Thank you. Truly," Friday said, tears filling her eyes at the generosity of strangers.

***

"Well, that was a great haul," Chuck said. "Since we didn't have much, it didn't take long to swap everything over. A whole new wardrobe and disposable diapers for the kid, and a case of assorted home-canned goods. What more could anyone ask?"

"How about a destination?"

"Wolf Whistle, West Virginia," Chuck replied snappily, a grin wide on his face. "Hey, Pastor Baker was all over the place before settling down in Georgia.

"What's the holdup?" Friday asked from the back.

"Looks like a roadblock. Go ahead and strap her in, then sit up here with me. I don't know what the law is about babies and car seats around here."

Friday anchored Ria's car seat to the floor brackets and climbed up front. "Yup, it's a roadblock. That's the good thing about not doing anything wrong: you can't get busted."

Chuck pulled to a stop and the officer stepped up to his window. "Good morning, sir, miss," he said. "There's a fugitive in the area. A convicted murderer escaped from prison six months ago but was spotted nearby last night." He handed the flyer to Chuck. "Have you seen him?"

Friday leaned closer to see and they both gasped, "Harvey," at the same time.

"Yes, that's one of the names he uses. So, I take it you saw him?" he asked, pen and notebook in hand, ready to take notes.

"You might want to look at hospitals and clinics," Chuck said. "He sort of had a kidney injury – left side. I told him there was nothing he could do about it, but I don't think he's the kind of guy to listen to anyone."

"What? Are you a doctor or something?" the cop asked.

"Yes," Chuck said, then pursed his lips, not comfortable about elaborating.

"So, did you examine him?"

"Nope, but I am the one who punched him. He came to our site and started tearing things up, threatening us. He was limping pretty bad when he left but was able to walk. You said he was a murderer?" Chuck asked.

"Serial murderer," the officer said, flipping through his notebook. "He was severely homophobic. He'd ask a guy out on a date and then, wham!"

"Wham?" Friday asked and looked over at Chuck.

"Tortured his victims until they died. That guy was sick. I won't

36

go into details – the lady being here and all – but let's just say he was a technicality away from getting the death penalty. He has the rest of his life sentence to serve in Florida. Knowing about the injury will definitely help. Anything else?"

"He was dressed in tight denim jeans and a white tank top," Chuck added. "Oh, and was wearing Wellington boots and was walking."

Friday put her hand up, recalling the stumbling adversary. "Or trying to. In other words, he was on foot. We never saw a vehicle."

"Yes, I think that's about it, Officer," Chuck said. "If you have a card, I'll call if I see him again. I certainly don't want his kind walking the streets or cruising the parks."

"You and me both," the cop said, giving Chuck a sly wink, handing him his official card with his cell phone number and nickname scribbled on the back. "Give me a call, even if you don't think it's important."

"Hey, Pete!" an officer called out from ahead. "They caught him! We're shutting down the roadblock."

Chuck started to hand back the card then changed the gesture to put it in his shirt pocket. "Just in case something else pops up," he said, giving Pete a wink. He stepped on the clutch and shifted into first.

Thump. Thump. Pete tapped the side of the van, giving Chuck a personal farewell. "Take care out there," he called.

"Oh, we will," Chuck said. "We will."

Chapter 4: Wolf Whistle

Four years later
Wolf Whistle, West Virginia

"I can't believe she's only four and a half years old and can read like a third-grader," Friday said.

"Or an adult from these neck of the woods," Chuck said.

"Yeah, it's sad that the education system can't be more stringent on school attendance. The teachers try, but if they can't get a kid's butt in the seat, it doesn't make a difference."

"Yup, an endless circle of poverty. These folks are so far off the government's radar, we can't even get welfare or disability insurance for those who qualify!" Chuck picked up his spiral-bound journal with names and clients, dates and procedures. "I've tried and tried, but they don't want to get a social security number. 'My daddy and grandpappy never had one and they did just fine. What do I need one for? Just to pay taxes?' If I've heard that once – or a variation of the same – I've heard it a hundred times."

Friday looked down her nose at him.

"Well, I hear it at least a couple of times a month," Chuck amended. "So, what do you have for me today?"

"No clients yet. In case you haven't noticed, we're running out of canned food. However, we still have that hen that hasn't laid an egg in a month or more. Sounds like chicken and dumplings for dinner," Friday said, brandishing the hatchet, checking the cutting edge for nicks.

"Damn! I wish I'd never asked you to show me how to butcher a chicken," Chuck said and took it from her.

"Hey, I'll do it if you want to gut it, pluck it, and cook it."

Chuck turned around and started walking to the hen house "Which one is she?" he asked, certain that she was following him. "I don't want to get the queen of four-egg omelets by mistake."

"This is the one, Daddy," Ria said, holding the chicken upside

38

down by the legs. "I caught her for you. Can I kill her?"

"Uh, no. Sorry, honey, but I don't trust your aim. I know you can hit a target on the tree with this thing," Chuck twirled the hatchet in his hand, "but since I'm the one who'd be holding down her head, I'm going to have to pass on that until you're a little older."

"You won't have to hold her; I can do it by myself. Watch this, Daddy." Ria put the chicken on the chopping block breast first, then pulled the legs back to get full body contact with the stump. With one hand, she held it down securely until it completely settled down. She then drew an imaginary line from the tip of the hen's beak forward – four inches long – then repeated it, a smooth rhythmic stroking movement. The hen was transfixed. Frozen. Dumb cluck hypnotized. "Can I do it, please," Ria begged.

"All right. Friday, get ready to chase it if she doesn't get a clean shot," Chuck said, handing his daughter the hatchet.

Thwack!

The chicken's head flew off with a well-placed blow. "I did it! I did it!" Ria squealed, jumping up and down, clutching the hatchet close as if it was her favorite toy.

"Whoa! Wait! Give me that hatchet. Our dinner escaped!" Chuck screamed. "Quick! The job's not done until you bring it to the table."

Not wanting to relinquish her prize tool, Ria scowled at him as if he was teasing her. Friday turned her around by the shoulders and pointed her in the direction the headless hen was running. "Go get it!" she said, patting Ria on the bottom to push start her.

Chuck took the hatchet from her and forty pounds of female vanished through the bush, chasing the headless chicken.

"Does that happen often?" he asked Friday as they stood back, watching the braided blonde grasp air, trying to catch the hen, then disappear around a clump of greenery.

"No, but it isn't that uncommon. Come on, let's help her. I don't want her to chase it into the blackberry bushes. I'd rather eat bullion and biscuits than climb through thorny brambles to get our chicken and dumplings."

"Ria! Ria!" they called out but didn't get an answer.

"How'd she disappear so quickly?" Friday asked.

"She's Ria," Chuck replied. "I refuse to worry until five minutes have passed." He looked at his watch. "I started counting two minutes ago. Ria! Ria! Come out, come out, wherever you are!"

"I'm over here, Daddy. Come help me."

"Oh, shit!" Chuck said.

"You're not supposed to say that," Ria called out.

"Are you okay?" Friday asked, ignoring her comment.

"I am, but he's not." Ria stepped out of the tumble of brush and onto the deer trail, dead chicken in hand.

"That's a she," Chuck said.

"Not the chicken," Ria said. "Him. He's hurt." She handed Friday the chicken and crawled back into the bushes. "Don't worry, sir. My daddy's a doctor and he can fix you up, good as new."

Chuck got on his hands and knees and followed her into the temporary shelter. There lay a beautiful specimen of man, handsome in just about every way except the grimace on his face, his five o'clock shadow more of a five-day shadow, his cheeks hollow from dehydration.

"I won't trouble you with asking if you're okay because I can see that you're not. I will ask if you can walk, though."

The man shook his head biting his chapped bottom lip in defeat.

"Friday, go back to the clinic and grab the cot. We'll use it as a gurney. Ria, go with her. Put that chicken up high where that stray dog can't get it, then bring me a bottle of water – a small bottle, not a jug." He turned to the man. "Save your breath. Don't even try to talk until we get you a drink. We'll have you fixed up in no time."

The man nodded again, his eyes squeezed tight as if to cry. But there were no tears. He was too dehydrated.

A minute later, they were back. "Here's the cot," Friday said, lifting up the aluminum-framed camp bed. "Do you need a hand getting him onto it?"

"We'll see." Chuck maneuvered the cot into the shelter the man had been living in, covered in leaves to keep warm. "Now, I'm going to roll you onto this. Are there any open sores or broken bones I need to watch out for?"

The man shrugged his shoulder, nodded to his kilt-covered crotch, then shook his head.

"Hernia? Sore balls or groin?" Chuck asked.

The man's eyes widened as he nodded in affirmation.

"Lots of pain?"

He kept nodding.

"I think I can help with that. As my daughter said, I'm a doctor."

"Here you go, Daddy," Ria said, reaching in with a bottle of water. "And I made sure the dog couldn't get the chicken."

"Thanks, dear." Chuck turned to his patient and said, "Just a dribble on the lips. I don't want you to sit up. That'll cause more pain. I can only give you a little at a time or you'll just throw it up. That's more pain for the hernia and more dehydration for the body."

Chuck wiped a few drops onto the man's full lips, moistening them so they wouldn't crack further. His mouth parted, ready for more. "Just a little…" He dropped in about a tablespoonful, then put the cap back on the bottle and handed it to Ria.

"Let's do this. It's going to be uncomfortable for a bit, but we're just a hundred yards or so away."

Chuck rolled his patient onto his side to make more room, settled the cot close to him, then rolled him back onto it. "Easy peasy," he said, noticing the man's grimace but lack of audible complaint. "Ready for this, Friday?" he called out to his waiting assistant.

"I can take this end without having to crawl in," she said. "Just say the word."

"Just a sec. Ria, crawl out and hold back the brush. Now, sir, are you ready?"

The patient nodded. His prayers had been answered.

"On two," Chuck said. "One, two!"

With a practiced coordinated effort, the four-footed ambulance exited the overgrown shelter, Ria doing her best to protect the man from the one stringer of blackberries that seemed to be everywhere.

"See, I told you I'd get help," she told the man as she walked beside him, doing her other job: distracting the patient from his discomfort.

"Ria, go get the door. We're taking him inside right away," Chuck said. His mind tumbled over whether he still had any sutures and where they'd keep the handsome Scottish stranger once they fixed him up. He wouldn't be able to hike home – wherever that was – for at least a few days. It looked like one more person would have to be fed with their meager rations.

An audible groan escaped from Chuck as he realized his last thought was a selfish one. At least one more person would live to see tomorrow because Ria's first chicken kill had escaped, causing her to find an injured man on the brink of death. A few ounces of food versus a man's life. No contest. "Thank you, Lord," he said audibly.

Chuck felt the man's hand on his. He couldn't speak, but the man could now smile in gratitude. "You're welcome," Chuck told him. "But you might not be too happy with me pretty soon. If you have what I think you have, surgery is needed. I have everything I need except a pain killer. Well, I have Ibuprofen but I'm not going to put that in your empty stomach. Are you ready for me to examine you?"

The man nodded and took his hand away, then stared up at the ceiling in the aging motorhome living room.

"Ria, go wet a washcloth with drinking water and let him suck on it, then stay up by his head. Friday, grab that prep kit we got last month. Team, we have ourselves our first major surgery."

"Lucky me," the man groaned, then passed out.

Chuck checked his carotid pulse and lifted the man's eyelids, making sure he was just unconscious and not dead. "Yes, I'd say you're lucky if you stay konked out for the whole surgery. I am going to assume he gave me permission to operate. Ria," he said, his daughter already back from her first task, "go grab a couple of drapes. Friday, it's time for this man to get his life back."

"Can I watch?" Ria asked.

Friday looked at Chuck, one eyebrow raised.

"She's not afraid of blood and knows anatomy better than most adults. I guess if she can't handle it, she can go outside," he said, then flipped the man's kilt up. "Ouch."

"Is that what a man's testicles are supposed to look like?" Ria asked.

"Nope," Friday said, then moved the kilt out of the way and unbuckled his belt. "This needs to come off. I'd say we have us a West Virginia Highlander."

"With a major inguinal hernia in his low lands region," Chuck added.

"I never saw a grown man's penis before," Ria said innocently, staring. "It's a lot bigger than little boys' penises."

"So is a man's nose," Friday said, her face pinched in concern. "Look at them someday. Little button noses on boys, big honkers on men."

"Let's get on with this before he wakes up. Now, no talking, Ria. I have to concentrate. I haven't done this in a while. And if someone comes to the door, you take care of it, all right?"

"Yes, sir," Ria said, her chest puffed in pride. "I'm you're best number two helper."

***

An hour later

"That went well," Friday said, wiping down the surgery implements, getting them ready for their alcohol bath. "How long do you think he'll stay out?"

"Not long. When you get done there, would you offer him that wet washcloth again? I didn't want him to suck on it while operating, just in case it revived him. Oh, and if it wasn't obvious to you, it looks like there will be four for your chicken and dumplings dinner. And for a few more meals after that. He won't be able to go anywhere for a while."

Friday looked back at the man, the most handsome man she'd seen in years. Rough-looking with his scruffy beard but with coal-black hair that she'd always found appealing. Her nether regions tingled, a feeling she hadn't experienced with the sight of a man in a long time. *Have my prayers been answered? Is it time for me to leave and my escort has just arrived?*

"Ria, where's that chicken?" Chuck asked, interrupting Friday's reverie.

"I hung her on the clothesline." Ria pointed out the kitchen window. "See?"

"Clever kid," Friday said, sealing the lid on the alcohol bath. "Since she butchered and caught it – in that order – I guess that means you get to clean it and I'll cook it, Dad. Ria, why don't you go see if you can find a stalk of wild celery for me? And when you get back, pick out some of the better-looking carrots and onions. We'll dress up the first dinner you supplied meat for extra nice."

Chuck held up his hands, inspecting the digits that had just held and reinserted a man's protruding bowels, repairing the tear in the scrotum they had intruded into. Then he looked out the window at the dead chicken, hanging on the clothesline, its feet secured together with one of his clean white socks. "A man for all seasons and hands for all reasons," he said, taking the filet knife from the butcher block. "Believe it or not, sometimes I miss fast-food restaurants."

As soon as he was out the door, Angus opened his eyes and looked around. An unexpected throat tickle startled him. He tried to hold his breath – he didn't want to cough – but that made it worse.

"Just breathe in to the count of four and exhale the same way," Friday said, quickly at his side, her hand firm on the bandaging, applying gentle pressure on his scrotum in case he did start coughing. "In, two, three, four. Out, two, three, four. Again, two, three, four. Out, two, three, four."

Concentrating on his breathing did the trick and the cough never materialized. Still afraid to speak lest it start again, he looked up and smiled weakly.

"Are you all right now?"

He nodded, then glanced at her hand, cradling his balls.

"Oh, I guess I can let go now," she said, blushing.

His grin widened and head canted to the side. 'If you have to,' he seemed to be saying.

"Here, let me get you some water." She started to set down the damp washcloth but handed it to him instead. While she was at the sink, she noticed him swipe the cloth across his face, then bring it to his mouth and suckle on it.

"Here, you'll get more from this," she said and brought the drink to his mouth, letting him sip the scant half cup of water. "I'm sorry we don't have any straws. We reused the ones we had until they split and were useless. We don't treat ourselves to a soda unless we go into town and that's not very often. It's not just because it's a lot of trouble to break up camp with all the ropes and tarps that make this place a clinic. We also need money for gas. Most of our patients pay for services with food or critters. We have enough fuel left to get to town but not enough for the return trip."

Angus reached for where his sporran should be – willing to pay for the services – then looked around nervously, realizing it and his money was gone. His kilt was, too, and in its place, a white bed sheet covered his loins.

"Oh, we didn't want to get blood on your plaid." She looked down at his dark brown boots, ornate with crossed leather straps and metal buckles, the soles thick with tire tread that had been cut to size to replace the original leather. "I'm sure glad you weren't wearing jeans. I don't think we would have been able to get them off over those boots."

He looked back to the water cup, one eyebrow raised.

Friday answered his unspoken question. "Give it a few minutes. If that little bit stays down, I'll give you more. Oh, and we're having chicken and dumplings for dinner. You're invited."

His mouth opened to speak then closed quickly and morphed into a scowl.

"Well, I hope you didn't plan on popping in and leaving right away after surgery. How long were you out there?"

Angus put up three fingers.

"Three days? Good Lord, man. It's amazing you're still alive!"

"I'm a Scot," he said, his voice rough, low, and heavily accented.

"Well, I sort of guessed that by your dress." She saw his glare and tried again. "Dress as in attire, not dress as in skirt. So, is there a Scottish settlement around here?"

He looked to the water cup again and grinned.

"So, you'll talk if I give you more water?"

His grin continued, his eyes now bright as he nodded.

"You're behaving more like a wily Leprechaun. And before you ask, no, we don't have any marshmallow bits." She gave him another half cup of water, enjoying the view of his strong frame as he shifted beneath the sheet. Now she was even more intrigued with him. *Don't get emotionally involved. A good-looking body is what got you in trouble the first time around!*

"Angus McDermott, at your service," he said, his accent thick and sultry. "And yes, my grandsire was Irish. Yer not the first to notice the wily trait. Our wee settlement is a two-hour hike over the hill if a person's in fair health. I heard of yer husband's healing clinic from some travelers coming through. My sister insisted I come see if he could cure my problem."

Friday's hands waved in front of her face, trying to erase some of what he had said. "First off, he's not my husband. And second, in a few days, you should be healed up enough to go back but not until then. And third, what about your wife? Why did your sister send you?"

46

"I havena a wife! Although my sister did say as to bring one back if I found a strong and capable lass. She's getting ready to drop her fourth child and could use a hand around the house and garden. So, that bein' said, does that mean you and the healer are betrothed?"

"No, we'll never be married," she said, blushing with a mixture of excitement and anger. The first man who's thrilled her in over five years, and he'd take any strong woman for a wife! But he *was* looking for one. Would he be better than sharing a double bed with a gay man? For a day or two, she'd like to give him a try just to get rid of four and a half years of sexual frustration. She looked back at his wonderous body, the ample balls and more than adequate cock that was sure to please once he had regained his health. Three or four days with him might be better.

Would he treat her as respectfully as Chuck, though? Not a certainty by any stretch, especially if he was old school. By his speech and attire, he was more than old school; he was Old World! And looking for a wife like he was considering what kind of milk cow to get! Get out of that fantasy, woman!

Stomp. Stomp.

The familiar sound of Chuck's footfalls on the steps brought her back to her senses. She'd stick with the commitment to Chuck that she'd made four and a half years ago, even if it had expired three years earlier. Safer. Plus, they wouldn't stay in this windy hollow forever. One of these days, folks would stop coming or he'd feel the call of exploring the next settlement down the road.

"Did I interrupt something?" asked Chuck.

"Ach, I'm too frail to be doin' anythin' worth interruptin'," the slightly flushed patient replied. "My apologies on my rude approach to yer homestead, me bein' so infirm that ye had to portage my frail carcass the rest of the way to yer clinic. I'd stand to greet ye, but I dinna think this lass wants me to be up and movin' around yet."

"She's a smart young medico and I trained her well. She's not a doctor or a nurse, but if I was sick or injured, I'd want her nearby,"

Chuck said, his hand out to shake his patient's.

"Angus McDermott, at yer service," he said, "although I seem to be more of a liability than an asset at this moment."

"We all have our weak moments," Chuck said. "It seems my daughter found you just in time. Another few hours and you would have died from dehydration. Speaking of that, would you like more water?"

"He's had a full cup and kept it down," Friday said, refilling his water glass. "I do think that keeping his intake to clear liquids for another couple hours would best. By the time I have our chicken dinner done, he should be able to have a Ria-sized portion."

"What's a Ria?" Angus asked, his eyes shifting back and forth suspiciously.

"I am!" Ria said, popping up at his elbow. "I'm the best chicken rancher in West Virginia," she bragged.

Angus started to debate her claim with stories of his nephew, then suddenly felt weak and wobbly despite the fact that he was barely sitting up. "Ye certainly are," he said and scooted his elbows back to his sides and lay down all the way. "If ye dinna mind, I think I'll take a little nap while dinner's cooking."

Friday and Chuck shared a 'look,' recognizing the post-surgery fatigue that comes after the initial elation of finding out the procedure was a success. "That would be a good idea," Chuck said and lay his hand on the man's forehead, checking for fever. None. "A body needs sleep to heal."

"Aye, then I'll do my best to follow the doctor's orders," Angus said, then shut his eyes and was out.

***

Two hours later

Angus's eyes fluttered open and he inhaled deeply. "Did I die and go to heaven?" he asked.

"Nope," Chuck said. "You're still in Wolf Whistle. How are you doing there?"

"My sniffer's still working. I never thought much about it, but if

48

angels cooked, I'm certain it would smell like this."

Thunk! Clatter! Thunk! Thunk!

"What's that?" Angus asked.

"Stay here with Angus," Chuck told Ria. "And don't let him get up or leave." He turned to the big Scot. "It's the wind. I have to take the tarps down or they'll rip to shreds."

"I'll give you a hand," Friday said. "Ria, set the table with bowls and spoons. Leave the glasses in the cupboard." She set the lid back on the pot. "Dinner will be delayed."

Chuck and Friday quickly and efficiently untied the ropes and bungees, dropping them to the ground so they could concentrate on folding the blue plastic tarps, holding them tight under their arms as they moved on to the next one.

A gust hit and knocked a branch from a tree, at the same time, blowing the tin from the top of the chicken coop. "Grab that!" Friday said. "It's our last piece!"

Chuck handed her his two tarps and wrestled the partially attached aluminum siding from the structure, cutting his hand in the process. "Damn!"

Friday rushed to his side to help and saw blood dribbling past his wrist. "Double damn! Give that to me and you take these and get inside. I'll be right there."

"What are you going to do with that?" he asked, ceding the metal to her and grasping his wound.

"Not let it blow away. Get inside. Now! That's an order!"

Chuck looked at her wide-eyed at her commanding tone. Never the meek one, he hadn't seen this side of her since they first met at Dr. Buddy's clinic. She was definitely taking charge right now. "Got it," he said, taking the last tarp and heading back to the motorhome.

Holding onto the three-foot-wide by eight-foot-long siding was like holding onto a heavy-duty kite in a mega-storm. Like a sail, the wind caught it and tried to carry Friday away. She wasn't going to let it go, though. Metal siding was a prized commodity in this region, and she and Chuck had worked hard to secure this piece. She wasn't going to let someone downwind get it for free. Finally, she got it under control then realized why. She was at the abandoned building at the end of their site, the one that used to be a smokehouse but had been condemned by the county. Shelter! She kicked at the lock at the door to no avail. Then she realized the hinges were older than the lock and hasp and kicked at them. Success. She wrangled the siding inside, then threw the door in there, too. They could deal with these hours or days later; whenever the blow was over.

Crap! Chuck's hand. I gotta get back!

Eyes squeezed shut as she headed into the wind, Friday didn't notice the huge branch flying right towards her. She didn't see it when it hit her, either.

Blindsided. Out cold on the ground and where Chuck wouldn't expect to find her.

***

"Let me help," Ria said, her hand hovering above her father's as he tried to wrap a temporary bandage across the cut in his palm.

"I got this," he said, then the gauze slipped again. "Okay. You win. Go for it."

Ria bit her bottom lip as she made sure the sterile strip didn't twist as she wound it around his hand. Finally done, she picked up the scissors. "Hold it tight," she told her father and cut the end. "Still got it?"

"Yes, Doc," he said, trying not to worry about Friday.

Ria snipped the trailing edge down the middle, then wrapped and tied the two pieces, securing the bandage. "Done!"

"I couldn't have done better myself," he said. "It looks to me like you have that magic touch. You're a natural healer. Now, I'll be back in a minute. I have to go find the cook!"

"Can I be of help?" Angus asked, uncomfortable at feeling useless.

"Yes. Stay here. Ria, same job. Make sure he doesn't go anywhere. One lost person is one too many."

Chuck opened the door and nearly had it ripped out of his good hand. He reflexively reached for it with his injured right hand, then stopped before following through. Stepping outside, he shoved the door closed but was unable to turn the handle to secure it.

"I got it," Ria said while he held it shut.

Chuck ducked low to keep from being blown about like that panel of siding, his eyes squeezed nearly shut to keep out pine needles and blowing debris. He traced the path from the chicken coop back to the RV. Nothing. Then he walked around their home to the back of their lot. Still nothing. He was headed up to the old brick smokehouse, his range of vision still limited, when he nearly stepped on her, hidden beneath a long-needle pine branch.

"Friday?" He bent forward to move the camouflage aside, then winced in sudden pain as he grasped it. *Damn! I'm going to have to put this hand in a sling. I can't stop reaching with it.*

Between using his foot and good hand, Chuck managed to uncover Friday, but he couldn't lift her.

The cot. If he could roll her onto it like he had Angus, he could haul it like a travois.

Back to the RV. The door was locked, though. He pounded on it. "Open up, Ria!"

The door opened with a whoosh, Ria catching it at the last second. She looked at him, alone and empty-handed, then looked behind him. "Where is she?"

"Let me in first." Chuck stepped inside and held the door with his good hand. "She's on the path. I need the cot you're on, Angus. Do you think you can get onto the couch by yourself or do you need help?"

"I can help him," Ria said, quickly at the recovering man's side.

Angus grimaced as he sat up, then rolled off, using Ria's shoulder as support. He didn't say a word, focusing all his attention on transferring himself. He managed to get situated on the couch, the sheet clutched in one hand at his side, the other grabbing the back of the sofa. "Done!" he proclaimed breathlessly.

"Ria, bring me the cot. I don't think I can do it by myself, so you'll have to help me. Angus, you'll have to live with the door open for a bit."

"Take the lass with you now," Angus said. "I'll bide."

Chuck held the handle as the wind blew the door open, his firm grip keeping it from slamming and breaking the window. Young Ria turned the aluminum frame cot on its side and dragged it to the doorway, leading it down the steps as her father grabbed the end, holding it tight against the gusts.

The father-daughter duo headed into the wind to find Friday, still unconscious, where the storm wreckage had knocked her down. Grabbing Friday by the hip, Ria pulled her best and only friend towards her as Chuck positioned the cot beneath her. "Let her go now," he shouted against the wind.

Chuck watched as Ria released her gently, her grimace of fear making her look more like her mother, Grace, than ever. A few minor adjustments and they had her settled. He stepped to the head end of the cot. "Come up here and help me pull," he said. "We're not going to carry her like we did Angus."

A tailwind assisted the two on their return to the RV, storm debris gratefully blowing out of their faces instead of into it. They stopped where their awning had been. The door was still open, thumping and banging it against the RV's siding as gusts relented then slammed it anew. Angus was upright, standing in the doorway, his kilt now belted on. "Just in case ye needed some lightweight help."

Chuck grunted then bent to the task of getting an unconscious woman up two steps with only one good hand.

Friday's head and shoulders suddenly lifted. "What happened?" she asked, her weight shifting as she tried to sit up.

"Hold on!" Chuck ordered. "Ria, set it down."

Chuck rushed to Friday's side, his eyes wide with fear. "Can you climb the steps?"

"Of course, I can," she said. She started to sit up, then swooned.

"Oh, shit!"

"You're not supposed to say shit," Ria said, looking back and forth between her two parental figures, making sure she wasn't going to get in trouble for repeating the forbidden word.

"You're right, sweetheart," Friday said. "It's okay in an extreme circumstance, though." She turned back to Chuck. "Let me try this again."

This time, Friday moved slowly, one hand on Chuck's shoulder to steady herself as she sat up. "I got this."

Another concerted effort and she was standing mostly upright, hunched over to stay on her feet as the wind gusted to near hurricane force. Holding onto Ria's shoulder, she climbed the steps. Chuck stood behind her, holding tight to the cot, so it didn't fly away. He didn't want Friday to try and chase it down, too!

"Angus, I think you can handle this much weight. Pull this inside, would you?" Chuck asked, pushing the cot upright through the doorway, grateful for the momentary lull in the wind.

Once inside, Chuck pulled the door closed and secured it with the deadbolt, the only other way to keep the wind from grabbing it open. He turned to Friday. "Well, did you save the tinware?" he asked sarcastically.

"Yes," she answered in the same tone. "As a matter of fact, I did. I also got that old brick smokehouse door opened. It's empty. Now we have a storm shelter in case we ever need one."

Angus and Chuck both snickered at the same time. "Like now?" Chuck asked.

"Maybe. How's your hand?"

Chuck held up the bandage. "Ria's a natural. Fixed it up just fine."

"Did she put stitches in it, too?"

"I didn't have time," Ria said. "Besides, he wouldn't let me. He missed you and went out to find you, almost before I even had it tied off."

Friday looked up at Chuck, his everpresent small flashlight in hand, ready to check her pupils. "Why?"

"Duh! Because I care. Now, chin up."

Chuck flashed the light in both eyes then repeated the gesture to verify his first conclusion. "Hmm. I don't like that, but there's nothing I can do. You have a concussion. I don't want you sleeping for more than an hour at a time. You'll probably be cursing me by morning for waking you up all night."

"No more than you'll be cursing me for making you."

"I can do that," Angus said. "I'm a light sleeper when need be."

Chuck frowned – ready to tell him no – then thought of how he'd feel if there was chaos all around and he wasn't allowed to help. "I don't think you'll pull on your stitches with nudging her shoulder. Looks like you get my spot in bed. Ria, I'm sleeping with you."

Ria tried to temper her excitement. She hadn't slept with him in ages, and he'd never slept with her on the pullout bench that served as dinner table seats ever! "All right," she said, swishing her smile into a serious look. "Just make sure you don't drink a lot of water before bedtime. I don't want you peeing the bed."

Friday and Chuck laughed, then Angus realized it was a joke and joined. "I promise," Chuck said. "Now, is the stew hot enough to add the dumpling dough yet?"

"Can I do it?" asked Ria.

"Might as well," Friday said. "You've proven your worth as a meat provider, search and rescuer, medic, and ambulance driver. We might as well add chef to your resume."

***

"So, this is where you two sleep and yer not..." Angus was stilled from completing his comment by a sharp elbow.

"My personal life is none of your business. Now, shut up and let me sleep." Friday pulled one of the many afghans they had acquired as payment for services over her head, trying to shut out both the noise of the storm still raging and the queries from the hot guy nestled inches away from her.

"Yer shiverin'. Here, let me…" Angus scooted closer, snuggling up to her back, and wrapped his arm over her waist.

"Knock it off," she hissed. "Don't you know a woman means it when she says no."

"But I dinna ask ye a question."

"And I didn't ask for you to cuddle, either. How would you like it if a big old black bear just walked up and laid its paws on you?"

"What are ye talkin' about, woman? That blow to the heid scrambled yer brains."

"Just because I'm a woman and lying near you doesn't mean I'm up for grabs to you or any other male who happens by. An unwanted hand is just as uncomfortable as a bear paw and potentially just as disastrous."

"I was jest tryin' to keep you warm. I wasna trying to compromise yer virtue."

"Just let me sleep."

"All right…Say, what is yer name?"

"Just call me Friday."

"Like the day of the week?"

Rather than explain the relationship of Robinson Crusoe and his helper, Friday, to a man who probably had never read the story, Friday grunted, "Yeah," and hunkered down, asleep before she thought again about how close he was to her.

"Friday," Angus said, pushing her shoulder even harder. "Wake up!"

"Huh?" she asked sluggishly, drool slipping out of the corner of her mouth. She brought her hand up to wipe it and missed, hitting herself in the eye instead. "Crap."

"Are you all right?" he asked.

"I don't know," she slurred. "No," she amended after hearing herself. "Get Chuck."

"I'm here," Chuck said, laying his hand on her forehead. He looked up at Angus. "Sort of hard not to hear everything when you're just a few feet away, despite the noise outside. No fever. I think you might be dehydrated. You're skin's too dry. When was the last time you had anything to drink?"

"Just whatever was in the chicken and dumplings. Before that, I don't remember. But you're right," she said, smacking her lips. "The salt in the soup would have sucked out water from my cells. If you don't mind, would you get me a drink of water?"

"Got it," Ria said, handing her an oft-reused water bottle.

The three watched as Friday chugged the whole bottle down, then handed it back to Ria. "Now, let me get some sleep. And if you don't mind, Chuck, let's try that new theory about letting the concussion patient get plenty of rest. I don't think I'm going to slip into a coma. I'm simply exhausted."

Chuck looked over Friday at Angus who shrugged his shoulder. "Should I let ye have yer place back?"

"Nah. I'd rather you sleep with her than on the floor or cot. Let's all get some sleep. Maybe the blow will be over by morning."

"Not likely," Friday mumbled, then snuggled back into the afghan.

The next morning, Angus gently nudged Friday's shoulder, testing for life and alertness. She responded with a quick snort, then rolled over, hands tucked under her chin, her face in his chest. Her nose twitched as she unconsciously sniffed a new smell. "What the…" she hissed, bounding out of bed in one swift movement.

"I dinna mean to startle ye," Angus said. "I jest needed to get out to use the privy. I dinna think it would do Chuck's surgery any good to climb over ye."

Friday looked over Angus and saw Chuck was in bed with them, fast asleep, snuggled next to him. "What's he doing there?"

Chuck awoke at the sound of Friday's voice. "Oh, sorry. Ria was kicking so much that I wasn't getting any sleep. You and Angus were only using half the bed, so I didn't think you'd mind. Sorry. I thought I'd be up before anyone noticed."

"Well, you two wait there. I get the bathroom first," Friday said, trying to keep her grin contained.

In bed with two gorgeous men. So what if one is gay? Chuck needs someone, too. Oh, crap! What if Angus is gay? Would he stick around? Would Chuck decide it was time for me to hit the road? Shut up! No thinking until at least one cup of coffee has been consumed.

Friday came out of the tiny bathroom to Ria waiting, her knees held close together in bladder urgency. "My turn," she said. "The guys went outside."

"Good for them. I'll get breakfast started."

Stomp! Stomp! Stomp! Stomp!

"I guess the wind did die down some," Friday said once both men were inside.

"Minimal damage since we got our tarps down in time. I took a look at the old smokehouse. Definitely usable space. You look better. How's your speech?"

"If Peter Piper picked a peck of pickled porcupines, how many prickles would he get?"

"That's not how it goes," Ria said, giggling.

"Okay, how's it supposed to go?" she asked.

"If Patsy Perkins poached a pool of purple poodles, how many puppies would she get?" Ria replied. "Beat that one, Daddy."

Chuck took a deep breath, searching for words with the letter P to swap around into a nonsense riddle, then blew it out. All he could think about was how great it felt being close to another man. A fairly healthy man who aroused desires in him that he had hoped were dead. Nope. Although he loved Friday, she didn't arouse him. He didn't love Angus any more than any other person who happened upon his clinic in search of medical assistance. But he certainly reawakened his desires. *Damn!*

Angus looked back and forth between the couple who weren't a couple. Suddenly it was clear as a freshly washed window. Chuck was like his Uncle Fergus: he liked other men. He sighed in relief. No competition for the lovely lady who was also a fine healer and decent cook.

Waiting until Chuck had left outside with Ria, Angus asked, "So, Ria isn't yer biological daughter?"

"Nope. My daughter is gone. I've been helping Chuck with Ria since she was born." Friday looked at Angus and saw he was intense, studying her as if he had more questions. "She's his, not mine, but we both love her. Any other questions?"

"Only one. It probably isna the last time I'll ask, but this is the first time. Will you marry me?"

"What?"

"All right, the second time, then," Angus said, his smile wide and infectious as he started to repeat himself.

"No, no. Don't bother. Are you serious? You just met me! How could you ask a life-changing question like that? Am I just some prime breed of cow you want to bring home to help with your sister's kids and garden? If you're looking for a slave, you're in the wrong place. I've been one before and won't go back."

"Wait. What? You were a slave?"

"Pretty much. When you can't come and go at will and are expected to work at specific tasks for no more than room and board, then you're a slave."

"Or you live in the hills of West Virginia," Angus said. "So, I take it you'll give me yer answer sometime before I leave?"

Friday was surprised by the grin she felt on her face. "Yeah, sure. But not today."

"All right then. It may take me longer to heal than Chuck thought if yer not leanin' toward an aye answer. I may not be stubborn, but I am determined. And jest to keep you from wonderin' about my motives, it isna yer skills as a cook and healer that interest me. It's the wily woman who's trapped inside; the one who's been livin' with a girly man for four and a half years out of a sense of honor and duty to help him rear his bairn. She's been deprivin' herself of the joys of her own life; of findin' and bein' with a man who wants to make her feel like she was glad she was born with breasts and a womb."

58

Her grin disappeared into a slack-jawed gape of awe. She realized her mouth was hanging open and shut it. She swallowed, trying to compose herself at hearing such an honest and heartfelt evaluation of her situation, one that had escaped her even. "Then I guess it will be four for dinner again," she said, a timid smile now in place.

"Aye," Angus said, moving in close, one large hand held up. "And I'll keep my bear claws off of you until you ask for them."

Stomp! Stomp! Shuffle! Shuffle!

Angus and Friday moved apart, allowing room for Chuck and Ria to enter the compact quarters.

"Let me check your cut," Friday said when Chuck came in, glad for the distraction.

The two sat down at the kitchen table across from each other. Friday focused on his hand, carefully unwrapping the gauze bandage, aware without looking up that the men were checking each other out. Not a word was being spoken but with that realization alone, she knew they were 'chatting' with eye movements. She longed to watch them, to see what was transpiring, but she knew it would stop if she did. Evidently, Ria was too young to understand that unspoken universal language that came after being around men for years and having life experiences.

"She did a great job," Friday said, her head still down. "You're right about the stitches. We'll have to see if we can get more butterfly bandages next time we're in town. I'll clean it again and rebandage it."

"Can I do it?" Ria asked.

Friday looked up at Chuck. He pulled his gaze from Angus. "Excuse me?" he asked.

"Ria wants to do the doctoring on your hand again. It's up to you," she said.

Chuck finally looked down at the work she had done. "Looks good to me. Ria, why don't you clean it up again then rewrap it?"

Ria looked at Friday and grinned. *Dad's being silly. He wasn't listening, huh?*

Friday nodded. "If you need help, honey, let me know. You got this. You're a natural. Just don't go treating anyone other than family and always get permission, all right?"

"All right. Now, Daddy, this might feel cold..." Ria looked up at her father and saw he was staring at Angus again. His eyes dropped to Friday and he sighed deeply, as if he had just lost her.

Even a four-year-old could understand at least a little of the silent language of men. She looked at Friday and saw her look at Angus. She'd never seen her look at anyone else like that. Was that why Daddy was sad? Was Friday going to leave with Angus? Ria felt her eyes get misty, tears starting. *Focus on what you're doing! That's what Daddy and Friday always said. It may be hard, but if you focus on the procedure and don't think about how difficult it is, you'll get through it faster and better.*

Ria picked up the roll of gauze from the tray Friday had set beside her. She wrapped her father's hand gently. He would still be with her. He'd stay with her forever...

Focus! Another three wraps and she was done. Handing her the scissors, Ria looked up and saw her father was looking at her now, not Angus. *Yes, he'll stay with me my whole life, even after I'm grown up. I'm his helper now. I'm his Friday.*

***

"Friday, why don't you check Angus and make sure there isn't an infection starting," Chuck said, not expecting her to refuse. "I'm going fishing with Ria."

"You're what?"

He chuckled softly at her surprise. "Hey," he said, coming up close so only she could hear, "I'm sure he'd rather have you check his balls than me. He likes you. You'll be safe without me. Besides, I really don't think he's the type to take advantage of you. He's a big man in many ways, a gentleman being one of them."

"How do you know that?"

"We *talked* while you were checking out my hand."

"Yeah, well, I was wondering what you two were chatting about. I had the feeling it was about me."

"Ria asked me about it later. Even she picked up on his attraction to you. She asked if the right woman came along, would I leave with her or could she come with me."

"Oh, Lord..."

"Yeah, well, she did say she was positive I'd never leave her. She was also just as sure you were going. Whatever you decide to do is fine with both of us. Has he asked you to marry him yet?"

"How'd you know?"

"Like I said, we 'talked.'"

"Go ahead and go fishing," Friday said, a pink blush rising. "I'll check his incision, then putter around here, cleaning up some of this storm mess. If he's up to it, we might string up the tarps again."

"Well, don't let him get too carried away. You can tell him I said not to do anything that hurts or strains. Remember, he's probably still weak from dehydration and lack of food for three days. Don't make him work too hard."

"No worries there."

Chuck looked at Friday and shook his head. "So, did you answer him?"

"What? About getting married? Come on. Get real. I haven't even known him for twenty-four hours and you expect me to make a lifetime commitment?"

"You made a four-and-a-half-year one to me and Ria with less. If I had been – shall we say, wired differently – we'd probably still be together."

"I haven't even left yet and you're already writing me off," she said, scowling in embarrassment.

"Did you hear what you just said?"

"I haven't even left and..."

Chuck raised his injured hand, stopping her. "You said *yet*. You've already made up your mind but don't realize it. Yet."

He looked up. Angus was standing in the doorway, listening to their exchange. "Turn around, Friday," Chuck said. "You have a patient to attend to and Ria and I have fish to catch."

Ria ran up and hugged Friday around the middle. "I love you, Friday," she said, then ran to her dad, sniffing back tears. "Come on, Daddy. We have fish to catch."

Friday looked up at Angus, his face unreadable. "Well, that was awkward," she said. "Go inside and lie down. I want to check your stitches."

Angus sat on the edge of the bed he had shared with her the night before, his hands in his lap. Trying to calm his excitement before she examined him, his mind went over all the gory scenes he'd seen in life: the slaughter of farm animals, the sight of his sister giving birth, and then he found his dick-softening image.

Overwhelming grief overtook him, the memory of his wife and child lying together in a coffin, blue-toned skin, grim-faced, their skin hard to the touch.

"Are you all right?" Friday asked. "You look like death warmed over."

He took a deep breath, trying to calm the tears that were coming, but it was no use – two had already escaped.

"It's okay," she said, putting a calming hand on his shoulder. "You don't have to be bashful. It's nothing I haven't seen before."

He chuckled, coming out of the misery and ugliness that was his past into the beauty of the present and hope of his future. Friday.

"Well, *this* is different," Angus said, not even trying to soften his thick accent. "Before, you were a healer. Now, yer the woman I asked to marry me. I'm havin' some trouble keepin' my excitement down." He looked down at the bulge that had started again at her touch, covered by his large hands but still obvious.

Friday swallowed audibly. They were alone for at least an hour. Was she afraid of him? No, he had told her he wouldn't lay a hand on her unless she asked. That was what she was afraid of. She was afraid of herself.

"Let me check out the incision first," she said, trying to keep the breathlessness she felt out of her voice.

Angus lay back on the bed, keeping his cock covered with his tartan, exposing the area that had been repaired with stitches. Her touch was soft and gentle, her hands warm and caring. Blood surged, causing his shaft to pulse and harden even more. "Christ, woman! Yer drivin' me mad. Is it or isn't it healin' properly?"

Friday pulled the tartan over her exam area, inadvertently creating an obscene tent. "How are you feeling?"

"Horny as a stallion in a corral full of fillies." He put his hands under his hips, keeping them under control but also creating an even larger presentation of manly prowess. "If I dinna sit on my hands, they'd be all over you. I've never felt such a draw to a lass. Do you want me to ask again or will you jest answer aye and we can get on with it? We can find a priest or parson or justice of the peace later. I promise I'll provide fer you, never let you go hungry or cold. I'll give you as many bairns as you want, too. I see the way you look at wee Ria. You do want yer own, aye?"

"Aye," Friday said, then lay down beside him, looking into his dark blue eyes. "I think I told you I had a daughter before. I'd like at least two or three more. A son here and there might be nice, too."

"Well, we can start on it right now," he said. "I did overhear Doc tellin' you not to let me do too much. If I start to ailin', I'll have you here by me, ready to fix me again."

"Oh, I don't think you'll need fixing. Here, let me take off your plaid. We have at least a while before they get back. Oh, and if you change your mind after being with me right now, it's okay. I won't be offended."

"Oh? Well, I'll be mightily offended if you change yer mind! I may be a bit fast the first time, me not havin' had a woman since my wife died three years ago, but the second and third time should serve you well."

"Well, if that's the case, let's get started. But be gentle. It's been over six years for me. I may have reverted back to being a virgin!"

Two hours later

"Hold on there, Ria," Chuck said. "Let's stay out here for a while. I want to cook these over a campfire. They taste better."

"But can I go in and tell Friday I caught six fish?"

"Nope. We'll surprise her. She'll come out when she's ready. She might be seeing to Angus's needs. Why don't you sing the periodic table of elements for me while I get it started?"

"Again?" she asked. Seeing his scowl, she began, "There's hydrogen and helium, then lithium, beryllium..."

"You know, you're lucky, Ria. Not many kids have the opportunity for a great education. Their parents may be smart, but too often they don't take the time to share their knowledge. One of these days, you'll thank me for being such a tough taskmaster."

"Hey, there," Friday said, standing in the doorway, Angus close behind her.

Chuck looked up and noticed the difference immediately. He sighed with a mix of frustration and loss at the change in his best friend. She was definitely committed to the man who had come to him in need of medical repair. If the nearness of the two – inside each other's personal zones – wasn't enough to say they had just enjoyed each other's bodies, their identical grins of satisfaction would have. Angus had convinced her, body and soul, to be his.

"Are you all right, Friday?" Ria asked. "You look kind of funny. Actually, you both do."

"I'm fine," Friday said. "I'll get a frying pan. Looks like we're cooking fish outside today. God, I'm glad it's summer. I can't stand the lingering smell of frying fish inside."

She turned around and Angus smiled at her, letting her pass. He resisted the urge to pat her bottom. It didn't make a difference, though. She was his and they both knew it.

Ria's narrowed look of distrust at Angus hadn't faded. Angus saw it and explained, "Ria, I've asked Friday to marry me and she said yes. We'll be leaving soon."

Ria took a deep breath, ready to protest, but knew it wouldn't do any good. She'd learned a long time ago – at least last week – that you couldn't win an argument with an adult. They always won. "Well, you be good to her," she said, then bent down to add more sticks to the fire her father had started, hiding her face so the others wouldn't see her tears.

"I promise to be good to her. Thanks for taking good care of her for all these years. Now, it's my turn. I promise you, I'll cherish her." Angus walked over and lay a gentle hand on Ria's head. "Truly."

***

"That was a fine dinner, Chuck," Angus said, his arm around a blushing Friday.

"That wasn't just dinner," Chuck said, "so, don't try and fool us. Ria and I both know it was our last supper with Friday."

Friday reached out and put her hand on Chuck's arm, trying to soften his scowl. "What would you have us do, Chuck? What if it had been you who had found that perfect someone? I would have understood."

Chuck patted her hand, then picked it up and kissed it. "You're right. I guess it's sour grapes. I had my chance…"

Friday snickered, then changed it into a cough. "Wind's blowing the wrong way," she said, looking back at Angus who was rolling his eyes. Evidently, he had figured out Chuck's preferences in lovers.

Angus spoke up. "Friday said she didn't have much to take with her. She doesn't need any household goods because I have everything we need. She can tote everything in her James bag."

"That's gym, as in gymnasium, not Jim as in James," Friday said, then leaned in and kissed him on the cheek.

"Ew…"

"Knock it off, Ria," Chuck said. "Just because we don't do that doesn't mean others don't display affection in a physical manner."

Ria fought back her tears. She was hurting on the inside – like

65

her intestines were tearing apart –frustrated with discomfort at this new emotion and unsure of how to handle it. "Will you come back and visit us, Friday?"

Friday took a deep breath but Chuck cut in. "We're leaving, too, darling. Tomorrow we'll pack up and head on down the road."

"But...but..." Ria protested.

"But what?" Chuck said. "Other than Angus, no one has come to see us in three days. Last week, it was only two old guys and I think they were just here to ogle Friday. We've fixed up everyone who needs it. I'm not going to stick around in this heat waiting for someone to get a fishing hook buried in a finger. Let's move north. At least as far as the gas in this ancient and ailing RV will take us."

"Speakin' of patients," Angus said, reaching into his sporran. "I never did give you payment for yer services. I ken it isna much, but I think it will help ye get a head start." He handed him a packet of folded bills. "A little extra as a dowry fer takin' yer helpmate and the surrogate mother of yer child."

Chuck glanced at the tidy bundle of bucks – a five-dollar bill on the outside – and put it in his front pocket without counting it. "Thanks. Every little bit helps. As far as your stitches go, they're the dissolving kind. If they start to bother you, Friday can take them out if you're healed. Friday, make sure you take a first aid kit with you. From what Angus alluded to, there are a few other people living in your new neck of the woods. They might need a hand, and other than myself, I can't think of anyone else more suited to working in these rough conditions."

"Can I go to bed now," Ria asked, her eyes skirting past Friday and Angus, focusing on her hero, Daddy.

"Why don't you help me clean up, and then we'll both turn in early," he said.

"I got this," Friday said. "You cooked, we'll take care of the dishes."

"I didn't come to break up yer family," Angus said, standing up gingerly. "And I may have jested about my sister tellin' me to bring home a wife, but it was jest that: a joke. I dinna plan on findin' such a fine person," he placed his hand on Friday's shoulder. Then he looked at Ria and nodded. "Or bein' felled by pain or rescued by such a courageous young lass."

Ria rolled her eyes in embarrassment then allowed a grin to escape. "Just don't take my daddy from me, too!" she exclaimed.

"No worries there," Chuck said. "No one on this earth could tear me from you. You'll have to be the one to leave, not me."

"I'll never leave you!" Ria declared, her bottom lip stuck out in defiance.

Chuck grinned at her devotion. "Not until you're eighteen you won't," he said, pulling her shoulders close to him for a hug. "You were too much trouble to get!"

Friday looked over at him, recalling their hasty exodus from the birthing clinic, Ria with both her triplet sisters smuggled away in her gym bag. "And you've been worth every frantic moment we spent," she said, piling the last of the dishes into her hands. We'll keep in touch, I promise. I don't know how, but we will."

Chuck reached into his pocket and pulled out a plastic business card. "There's only one person I keep in contact with. Silas will know where I am and how to find me. Here's his phone number and address."

Friday turned around, her arms laden with plates. "Put it in my back pocket. I won't forget it."

Angus stepped between them, intercepting Chuck's move to put his hand on his fiancée's fanny. "I'll take charge of this, if you don't mind," he said, taking the card and putting it in his sporran. "No one will get into this without me bein' awares."

Just don't keep it from Friday or there'll be hell to pay! Chuck choked back the verbal threat but knew it showed in his eyes.

Angus nodded. *Dinna worry. She'll have access to it. I willna keep her from you. If she wants to come back, she can. I'll make sure her life is so grand and full of children, though, she willna want to leave.*

Still facing Angus, Chuck shut his eyes briefly then opened them to stare. *You do that.*

"Are you all right, Daddy?"

"Just a little tired, dear." Chuck called to Friday inside the RV. "Just put the dishes in the sink. We're going to bed early."

The clatter of dishes on porcelain answered his request. Friday came to the doorway. "Then Angus and I'll go for a walk so we don't disturb you. Sleep well. We'll see you in the morning."

Yeah, right. You'll be gone before daylight. I know I would.

***

The next morning, Ria woke up and looked around. "They're gone!" she exclaimed, then turned to see her father come up the steps. "Daddy, did they sleep outside? They didn't even say goodbye!"

"They said goodbye last night. At least, I believe they thought they did. Don't worry. I made sure I gave Friday the card for Silas. She's not out of our life. She never will be. She's part of both of us. She's the closest thing you'll ever have to a mother and knows it. I don't know when, but I do know she'll be back. Maybe not to live with us, but we'll see her again. Who knows, maybe she'll have more children by then."

"More children? I'm her only child."

"No, she had one before I ever met her. Her daughter was taken away from her. I doubt she'll ever get her back, but Angus wants to give her more babies."

"Why wouldn't you give her more?"

"It's complicated," Chuck said, then held her close. "Come on. Let's eat something, then pack up everything we want to keep. I'll put a 'free' sign on what we're leaving. Next time someone comes by to chit chat or have me check on a rash, they'll find it. They'll know it was our time to move to greener pastures."

"Greener pastures?"

"That's a phrase. When the cows or goats or sheep have eaten all they could in their area, the shepherds move them to greener

68

pastures. That means more grass to eat so they'll grow bigger and stronger. That's what we need."

"All right, but I think it would be better to say we're going where there are folks we can make stronger and healthier, not cows or goats."

"You're right. Oatmeal or cold cereal?" Chuck asked.

"Cold cereal, no milk. I don't want to wash more dishes."

Chuck looked at the sink. "Just like life, there's always a dirty dish to be washed. Let's get started."

He took off his watch and put it in his pocket, then felt the wadded bills Angus had given him as payment for services and dowry money for Friday. He pulled it out and unfolded it. The five-dollar bill had been wrapped around five one-hundred-dollar bills. "Whoa!"

"What's wrong?"

"We have money enough to go wherever we want and also buy food! Angus gave me dowry money…"

"Dowry money and what's wrong, Daddy?"

"I just realized something. The bride's family is supposed to be giving the groom the money, not the other way around. What I did for him wasn't worth five-hundred and five dollars!"

"Maybe the stitches weren't, but Friday's worth a lot more than that."

"Amen to that!"

Chapter 5: School Days

September 3, 1997

"Hello, Dr. Armstrong. My name is Thelma Ritter. I'm the school teacher in this district. Part of my job is to make sure all school-age children attend our classroom at least one day a week."

Chuck looked at the thin crone and shivers went up his spine. She looked as if she hadn't smiled in ten years, at least. A grin arose unexpectedly on his face. *So, that's where the phrase sour puss came from!*

"Did something I say amuse you?" she asked with a scowl.

"Nope. Just wondering how high your elementary school goes. As in, which grade level, not the ceiling height."

"Sixth grade," she replied, her chest puffed out in pride. "And I teach them all."

"Well, I appreciate the offer, but my daughter is homeschooled."

"Does your wife do the teaching?"

"No, I do," Chuck said, not wanting to disclose his marital status and have every single woman in the hollow chasing him.

"Are you a certified instructor?"

"No, but I am a medical doctor with more hours in college than any elementary school teacher I've ever met or heard of."

"Well, just because your fanny was in the classroom more than mine doesn't make you a better teacher."

"I agree, but just because you have a teaching certificate doesn't mean you're a better teacher, either. Tell me, do you have any sixth graders in your class right now?"

"Yes, I have one very bright young man."

"I'll tell you what, you create a standardized test and we'll give it to him and my daughter at the same time. If she beats his score, you'll leave us alone."

"But he's twelve! Your daughter is what, seven?"

70

"She'll be six in January – four months from today."

"No, no. That will never work." She glared at him, her doubts of success as plain as her pointy features.

"Of course, we'll both be in the classroom supervising. I wouldn't expect you to send the test home with her," Chuck said, his chin up with self-confidence.

"All right. I'll give them both the same test I give students before they can attend middle school. Shall we meet at the school at, let's say, ten o'clock?"

"That sounds good except for one thing," Chuck said.

"Yes…"

"Where's the school?"

***

The next day, Chuck and Ria hiked the half-mile to the school, leaving their home on wheels attached to the tarps and trees. "Is that it?" Ria asked, pointing to the small ramshackle building.

"Must be. There's nothing else around here, plus there's an old tire swing on that tree. The playground equipment, I suspect."

"Oh, there! If you look carefully, you can see that beat-up old sign. Butcher Hollow Academy." She got the giggles. "Academy?"

"Hey, be nice. Being smart won't get you near as far in life as good manners."

"Yes, sir. See, I can use my manners on you, too."

"I don't think she'll appreciate your sense of humor," Chuck said, trying to suppress his grin.

"Or understand irony," Ria said.

"That, too."

"Good morning, Mr. Armstrong. Ria," Ms. Ritter said, a tall tow-headed boy at her side.

"Excuse me," Ria said. "He's *Doctor* Armstrong."

The teacher glared at her, then softened the scowl into a fake smile. "Yes, yes, so he is. Welcome to our humble academy. This is Jim Bob Johnson, the sharpest young man I've ever had the pleasure to teach."

"You're only twelve?" Chuck asked the gangly youth with the blond peach fuzz mustache.

"I just turned thirteen on the Fourth of July," Jim Bob said, then looked at the teacher as if to ask if it was okay to tell the truth.

Ms. Ritter blushed at getting caught in the deception. "A month or two either way…" she said, then stepped back to let Chuck and Ria enter the classroom.

"Where are the other students?" Chuck asked.

"The whole lot of them is down with influenza," she said. "I told them to stay home if they were sick. We didn't need them to be spreading their germs around."

"Sound advice," Chuck said. He looked around the room and only saw six desks. "Where do you want Ria to sit?"

"Jim Bob sits up here next to me in front. She can pick any of the others as long as it isn't too close to him. We don't want eyes straying from their papers," she said, a sneer rising on one side of her face as she looked at Ria.

Chuck bit back his ire, his lower lip sucked in to keep from commenting.

"Don't worry," Ria deadpanned. "I'll keep my paper covered so he's not tempted," then allowed a self-righteous smirk to show.

Pride swelled in Chuck at her cleverness and ability to resist intimidation. "Here, Ria. Wipe the desk before you sit down. This year's influenza strain is particularly virulent."

Ria took the disposable wipe from him. "Yes, sir," she said, then bent to work, scrubbing the desk, hiding her wide grin.

Ms. Ritter ignored the jabs and handed out the papers. When offered a pencil, though, Ria politely refused it. "No, thanks. I brought my own." She held up a four-inch-long paisley-printed pencil. It was her lucky pencil, one of the last items she still had from Friday.

"I'd prefer…" Ms. Ritter began, then realized she was being petty, insisting that she use one of her standard yellow pencils. She looked up at the clock. "This is five pages of work pertaining to everything a student should know by the time he or she graduates from the sixth grade. You have one hour to complete the test. No bathroom breaks until you're finished."

"Isn't this the same one I took last June?" Jim Bob asked.

The teacher blushed crimson this time. "No, this is a different one," she lied, her eyes blinking rapidly trying to regain composure.

"Oh, okay," he said, then looked over at Chuck and shrugged one shoulder.

An awkward silence filled the room as both students stared at Ms. Ritter. Chuck finally said, "They're waiting for you to tell them they can start."

"All right, class," she said. "Begin. One hour is all you have. Wrong answers will count against you, so no guessing."

Ria bent to the task, whizzing through the math problems, double-checking the instructions. She raised her hand in the air.

"No questions," Ms. Ritter said.

"I think she's allowed one," Chuck countered. "She's never taken one of your tests. If it isn't appropriate, you don't have to answer it. Ria, what's your question?"

"Am I supposed to show my work on the math problems? It doesn't say?"

"Either way," Ms. Ritter said, then looked at Jim Bob, still working on the first question. "You know, there's a song we used to sing in our classroom to help us remember," she said, then looked at Jim Bob again, trying to get his attention.

The boy was intent, though, and didn't have time for her.

She started humming a tune, totally out of character for the prim woman, then Chuck realized what she was doing. "Hold on a minute," he said when he saw Jim Bob's eyes brighten. At hearing the tune, he quickly ran through the page, marking off numbers of the multiple-choice questions without even reading them.

"What's wrong?" Ms. Ritter asked.

"I'll tell you what's wrong," Chuck said, taking the paper off Jim Bob's desk. He looked at the boy and read the second question.

"Jim Bob, what's seven times six plus two?"

The boy's eyes squinted tight as he tried to visualize the problem.

Chuck turned the paper face down and said, "Go ahead and write it out if you need to."

Jim Bob did, but came up with an answer of forty-five.

"Okay, next question. If you had five cars and all had four wheels and two cars had six wheels, how many tires would you need? Go ahead and write it down. I can repeat it if you'd like."

Jim Bob tried, but couldn't figure it out. Chuck turned the paper over. "So, how come you got these answers so quickly?"

"Because this is an ABBACDCD test," he said.

"And how did you know that?"

"Because of the song Ms. Ritter was humming. It's a tool, she told us."

"Yeah, well, she's the real tool," Chuck said. "Ms. Ritter, how about giving me two other tests? One that doesn't have a song attributed to it."

"Done!" Ria said.

"But that was less than ten minutes," Ms. Ritter said. "How'd you get done so fast? Did you guess?"

"Nope. You said I didn't have to show my work. These were easy. Daddy gives me tougher tests. Do you want to check them or should he?"

"Here," the teacher said, snatching it from Ria's hand.

Ms. Ritter went down the page, chanting ABBACDCD as she went, verifying the coded answers. "She must have cheated."

"You're the only one who cheated," Chuck said. "And you're certainly not doing Jim Bob or anyone else any favors by giving them answer keys. Do you think life is going to give them cheats on how to survive in the real world? Or maybe you don't have faith that they deserve anything but a second-grade education? Nope, you're not getting my daughter into this school. As a matter of fact, I think you should be reported to the school district."

"No, no, don't do that. They can't get any teachers to come out here. I'm all they have."

"Well, then teach! I see books on the shelf. Teach them skills they can use in life. That was a great question about tires and wheels. Keep up with real-life situations and how to fix them. Tell them how to halve or double a recipe, how to balance a checkbook or fill out a job application. For God's sake, teach them to read!"

"Are we done now, Daddy?"

"Yes, we are. Jim Bob, nice meeting you. If you're ever in our neck of the woods, drop by and say hi. I have a few books you might want to borrow."

"Thank you, sir."

"Come on, Ria. Let's go see if we can catch a frog. It's time for a biology lesson."

***

Five years later – Lakeview, Pennsylvania

"Hello, Dr. Armstrong. I'm Harvey Taylor, the school teacher in this area. I'd like to invite your daughter to attend our school. It's a state law, by the way."

"Ria's homeschooled," Chuck explained, knowing this was going to be the same scenario it always was when they changed locations.

"Are you a certified teacher?" he asked.

"No, but let's make this quick for both of us. How about setting up an appointment for my daughter to take a grade placement test. Do your elementary schools graduate at the sixth or eighth-grade level?"

"Eighth grade around here."

"Fine. Let's meet at your school tomorrow at ten o'clock. If Ria passes your eighth-grade placement tests, you'll give her a certificate and leave us alone."

"But, sir, she's only ten, maybe eleven years old."

"Ten, but that doesn't matter. Are you willing?"

"Yes, sir. I'll see you tomorrow."

The next day, eleven o'clock

"Well, that one was easy," Ria said, brandishing her diploma. "Do you think they'll let me take the high school test?"

"Don't get cocky. You're not even a woman yet. We'll keep up with your studies. At least, the libraries around here are better than the ones in the backwoods. I'd love for you to attend at least one semester of real high school for the science labs they can provide. Plus, it wouldn't hurt for you to learn how to get along with kids your own age."

"But they're so boring," Ria said.

"Cluck, cluck, cluck," Chuck replied.

"Yeah, yeah, yeah. I'm getting cocky again."

"But so perceptive. Let's go grab our tackle and go fishing to celebrate."

"Ah, Daddy. You're so perceptive, too."

"Well, I can't think of any time you don't want to go fishing, but you're right. You get that from me."

Ria turned away and grimaced. He was a wonderful man – probably the most perfect one in the world – but he'd never talk about her mother. One of these days, though, she'd find out about her. Until then, she'd claim all the good things she had were from him. Her doubts and insecurities must come from her mother because he certainly didn't seem to have any.

Chapter 6: Thirteen

June 2005
Wolf Whistle, West Virginia (again)

Ria picked her way through the woods, following the deer path to the wide spot in the stream that historically had the best trout fishing. She had broken her fishing pole on her last expedition but had the reclaimed brass eyelet screws and line in one pocket, her Leatherman tool in the other, ready to construct a new willow pole. She always had a mint tin filled with fishing lures in her hip pocket, ready to tie on at dusk, the best time of day for catching trout.

She had taken to the trail early today, though. Something was going on. Daddy seldom asked her to 'make herself scarce' unless he felt the person coming to the clinic was a bad influence or was foul-mouth and without restraint. Or was a scummy lowlife who he feared might try to hit on her or make a pass.

She knew all about the facts of life – both the physical aspects and the social ones. Over the years, many battered women had come to them for help. They were usually distraught, totally without a filter on their explanations of how they had got so messed up, blathering on and on about what their man had done – or tried to do – to them sexually. Her father had explained to her early on that in a perfect world, the assaults would never happen. Almost every time, there was alcohol involved. A few times, they had packed up their home and clinic on a minute's notice, spiriting away a woman and her children to a relative in a different town, one time their trek taking them two states away.

It really was providence, Divine intervention, he explained. It was better to be fluid in their lives and help others than let the abuses continue. If they had remained where they were and simply sent the woman on her way, the man would probably figure out who had done the sheltering or relocating – the new guy in the area. Twice Daddy had been attacked by the angry spouse-type person.

The couples weren't always married, but the man always felt as if the woman was his to do with as he pleased. It didn't help that the children saw this and carried it on into their lives as adults. 'Daddy had to knock some sense into Mama' made sense to the boys. And the girls thought that was the way life was supposed to be, too.

"We have to help break the cycle, Ria. We fix bodies, but if we can fix spirits and lives, too, then we should. We're blessed to be so mobile."

And that was part of their problem today. The RV they had been living in since she was six-months-old was finally giving up. Metal fatigue was literally making it fall apart at the seams. The wind blew through every crack and crevice, bringing moisture with it when it rained or snowed. It was summer now, but they knew they had to do something before the freezing nights began in late September. The structure was too feeble to drive to another spot. The universal joint had fallen apart again, and this time, the driveline was so rotted out, a complete one would be needed to make it go again. The cost of one was more than the vehicle was worth.

And that's why Daddy had called Silas.

"If anything ever happens to me, you call this number," he said, showing her the plastic business card stuck to the refrigerator that was now just an icebox. It, like just about everything else, had failed. "I'm hoping he can find us out here. I've made arrangements for another home for us."

"Please tell me we're leaving this vacuum."

"Vacuum?" he asked.

"Yes, I swear it sucks the life right out of me. You know, when you blow hard over an object, it creates a vacuum? Well, the wind blows so hard here, it may not suck the life out of me, but it sure zaps the joy out of everything. Well, except for the fishing, and that's only in one spot."

Chuck looked at his watch, verifying the time of his inner clock. "Head on down and do some fishing. Give me an hour or two. Better yet, I'll come and join you later. He should be gone before dark."

"No worries," Ria said. She grabbed an apple from the counter, noticed it had a wormhole in it, then grabbed another one, just as marginal. "I'll make sure I cut it before eating it."

"The only thing worse than finding a worm in your apple…" Chuck began.

"Is finding half a worm," she finished. "I am so ready to leave!"

"Catch dinner first," Chuck said, then kissed her on the top of her head, his eyes open, checking for ticks. "And keep away from the bushes. Deer ticks are rampant this year."

Five minutes down the trail, the sound of a man crying brought Ria out of her introspection about life and where it would take her and her father this time. No matter what, it would be different. They would have a new home. She trusted him to figure out how they would leave this desolate valley and find a motorhome.

It was a young man, maybe eighteen but certainly no more than twenty, and he definitely wasn't from around here. He was wearing clean, unripped denim jeans, not frayed and work-worn overalls. His dark hair was short and appearance overall was well-groomed. She looked down and saw he was wearing bright white and red sports shoes, not muddy boots. Yes, he was a transplant, probably lost and that was why he was crying.

Ergh! Don't assume! Daddy said to get the facts first, then deal with the situation. Assuming makes you the first part of that word: an ass.

"Excuse me," Ria said. "Is there something wrong?"

Evan wiped his nose with the back of his hand, wishing he had long sleeves instead. He looked up and stared. "Stillwater?"

Ria looked over at the pool where she loved to fish. "Yes, it's still water. That makes for the best fishing. Watch," she said, hoping to distract him and get him out of his funk. She bent down and grabbed a fistful of sandy soil and tossed it into the water. *Plop, plop, plop.* "See? Nothing."

"No, that's not what I meant, but what are you doing?"

"When the time is right for the fish to feed, they'll be all over the place, jumping out of the water to catch the mayflies. You see, that's what they think that surface disturbance is: hatchlings. They come up to feed. At least, the trout do. Catching catfish is a whole different method."

"Okay. That's logical. But are you a Stillwater? You look just like our friend's daughter. I can't remember her name. I haven't seen her for a few years, but if you aren't her, you could be her twin."

"Nope. I'm not a Stillwater. And if I have a twin, my daddy never told me about her. So, is whatever was bothering you over?" Ria reached in her hip pocket and took out a red handkerchief and handed it to him. "Here, take this one. I have dozens at home."

"Thanks," he said and turned away to blow his nose. He turned back, started to offer it back to her, then realized how crude that was. "If you don't mind, may I keep this? I can pay you for it," he said, fumbling in his hip pocket for his wallet.

"No, I don't mind if you keep it, but I do mind if you try to pay for a gift. Lots of folks who come to our clinic pay in goods. We wind up with dozens of afghans and handkerchiefs, chickens and canned foods. We don't have money, but we keep fairly warm and well-fed. At least, we eat a lot of eggs. When the hens quit laying, then we get fried chicken or chicken and dumplings."

"And fish," Evan said, nodding to the long bare stick she held.

"Were you trying to fish here?" she asked, then sat down on the boulder next to him, not wanting to whittle her pole while standing. Besides, this was her favorite spot in the whole world. So far. She'd share it but didn't want to give it up.

"Well, sort of. I got mad a few minutes ago and threw the pole upstream as far as I could. I felt better for about ten seconds. Then I tried to retrieve it and got soaked." He stepped down on the ground and his shoe squished.

"Take off your shoes and turn them upside down. Loosen the laces first and pull the tongue and insole out so air can get inside. They won't dry completely, but by the time we get done fishing, your feet will be dry and the shoes won't be sopping wet."

"Sounds like the voice of experience," he said. "Oh, and I'm Evan, by the way."

"Evan by-the-way, I'm Ria Armstrong. My dad's the doctor around here. I'm his helper."

"Armstrong? Are you any relation to Papa Doc Armstrong?"

"I don't know. I never heard the name. The only relative I have is my father, Charles Darwin Armstrong. Folks who know him well call him Chuck. I only know his real name because that's what's on his driver's license."

"That's why we're here – to see a guy named Chuck. We drove a big ol' RV in here. I guess Silas is going to drive all of us out of here in it, back to the car I drove in. We caravanned into a little town about half an hour away. The roads were too rough to tow anything, even a compact car. I guess we're all going to leave via the RV. When we get back to the Bug, Silas and I will go back to hell. I mean, Massachusetts."

"Why did you say hell? And get back to what bug? That sounds more ominous than going back to hell!"

"Bug is the nickname of a car: a small Volkswagen car. Hell is because I don't want to face life anymore. My father died. Everywhere I go at home, I'm reminded of him, of all the fun he and Dad and I used to have. I literally hurt right here," Evan said, touching his breastbone.

"Are you sure you don't have a bruised sternum?" Ria asked, then sucked back her embarrassment. "Sorry. It's the doctor in me, always looking for a physiological answer to pain. I remember that pain now, though. I guess at one point, I really had a mother, but I don't remember her. I had someone in my life who was a mother figure, though. Friday and Daddy took care of me since the minute I was born. She left when I was almost five. They say you don't remember anything before that age, but I do. I barely remember her face, but I remember the pain of loss. You're right. It's smack dab in the middle of the chest."

"How did you get over it?"

"Time. Oh, and distracting myself with doing positive stuff. I mean, it may sound weird, but I work hard at learning everything I can. Daddy had been training her to be a medic and I was right alongside her, learning everything. I bugged him after she left to continue teaching me as if she was right there next to me. She was sort of my invisible friend. I knew she wasn't dead, and he promised me that I'd see her again someday, but I took what I could. Do you think you could do that for your father?"

"Yeah, I think so. At least, I know he'd be proud of me. Shoot, he was always proud of me. Both dads were, but Father was so sure I'd wind up a doctor, too. 'You're so much like me at your age,' he'd say. It was definitely encouraging."

"Evan, if he was alive right now, he'd be saying the same thing, I'm sure. You seem like a decent guy. Does that mean you're all alone now? What about your mother?"

"As I said, I had two dads. I'm down to one. Like you, I never knew my mother. My two dads adopted me when I was a few days old. They said I was their fifty-grand present to themselves."

"They bought you?"

"Yup. Hey, not many people start life having their worth practically pasted on their ass. I mean, butt."

"Ass is right in this situation. But, how can you have two dads? Isn't that illegal or something?"

"No, it's not illegal. Two people of the same gender can get married in most states in the union although it's still a capital offense in many countries. Where have you been all your life? You didn't know about this?"

"We've been in the backwoods since the day I was born, I think. If my dad didn't tell me or I didn't read it in a book, I didn't believe it. You'd be surprised at some of the nonsense these folks believe. Did you know that some of these women still believe that babies won't be conceived unless they're married? They're all sorts of confused to find out they're pregnant before the preacher comes around."

Evan chuckled. "Yeah, and it was probably the guys who told them that, too."

Ria laughed and pointed at him, "You're right! How long have you been around here?"

Evan looked down at his Rolex. "About an hour. You know, you're a great distraction. How old are you?"

Ria sighed, not wanting to let the sharp, handsome young man know she was so young. "I'm a high school graduate. I'm taking some correspondence college classes, but I probably won't graduate with a BS unless I go to a brick and mortar facility. That's one reason Daddy wants us out of here. He says this area is holding me back."

"Well, it looks like we're going to be around each other for a few more hours, at least. Why don't you show me how to fish with a stick?"

"Well, unless you're going to spear them, you need a hook and line, and preferably, a fly."

Evan looked up and focused on an imaginary house fly, then reached up and snatched the air. "Here," he said, offering it to her.

Ria took the pretend fly and put it in her mouth. "I'll keep it in here until I'm ready with the line," she mumbled as if her mouth was full.

"Ria," Evan said, laughing, "you make life worth living. I hate to say how miserable I was, but that all seems like a bad dream now."

Ria gulped, then laughed. "I accidentally swallowed it," she said, feigning a frown. "Don't catch another one until I'm ready."

Two hours went by, the young couple laughing and bumping shoulders at their jokes and silliness. When the sun got lower in the sky, Evan bent down and grabbed a fistful of sandy soil, then threw it where Ria had earlier. Suddenly the pool was alive with little fish mouths poking up, an occasional trout leaping completely out of the water. "Look at that!" he exclaimed.

"Shush," Ria said. "They're dumb but not deaf. Now, watch me." She whipped the pole with the string and bird-feather fly tied to it overhead, then let the lure settle on the surface. *Zap!*

"You got one," Evan whispered excitedly, "and on the first try, too."

"They're hungry tonight," she said, bringing the line in, hand over hand. "Normally, I let the first ones go, but it looks like it's going to be four for supper, so we'll keep them. Do you want to try?" she asked, setting the flopping fish into the shallow holding pool she had excavated years ago.

"I thought you'd never ask." Evan took the pole from her and tried to copy her smooth movement. "Don't laugh. This is my first time. I've fished before, but it was off the back of a boat in the ocean. Swordfish are tough to reel in, but this looks like more of a challenge."

"Only if you don't know what you're doing or fishing in the wrong spot."

Evan caught a twelve-inch trout on his second try. "Oh, my God! I can't believe it!" he hissed, screaming in a whisper.

Ria removed it from the hook and added it to hers. "Go for at least two more. They'll be biting for just a few more minutes, and then they're done for the day."

The fourth fish was a whopper: fifteen inches long, at least. Evan pointed the tip of the pole toward Ria for her to take off the fish and add it to the holding pool. Instead, she took a device out of her pocket, clicked it over his tail fin, then released it back into the main pool.

"Why'd you do that?" he asked.

"He's the old man of the pond. He stays here. I guess I should have let you punch his tail fin. When I release a fish back into the water, I mark him. It's just a hole puncher and I don't make a complete hole, just a little arc. I want to track how many times I've caught the same fish." She bent down to the holding pool and picked up a twelve-inch fish by the gills. "See his tail? I've caught and released him at least six times. A few times, I've forgotten the hole punch, but you get the idea. I kept all these today because from what it sounds like, this is my last time fishing here. Still, the old man needs to stick around."

"Wow, that's cool," Evan said. "So, do you think we should be heading back? The sun is getting low and I don't know my way around here. I guess I should have stayed where I was. Silas won't know to look for me here. Then again, Silas is known for his tracking skills. He can find anyone or anything with the slightest of clues."

"Silas Priest or Holmes?" Ria asked, chuckling.

"Priest, but he's a sort of Sherlock Holmes. So, I guess you've heard of him?"

"Slightly. I just know that if something happens to my dad, there's a card on the fridge with his name and number. I guess he's my escape from hell ticket."

"Funny, that's what my father told me, too. It's weird that we're connected that way."

"Yeah, weird," Ria echoed. She took out her Leatherman and gutted the fish, throwing the remains into the water.

"Isn't that polluting the water?"

"Nope, that's feeding the catfish and crawdads." She picked up a stick and ran it through the gills of the four large trout. "Here, you caught 'em, I cleaned 'em, and you can tote them back. I'll let Dad cook them. I want to meet this guy, Silas. I gotta know who he is and why I was kicked out of the clinic because he was coming. Something's fishy and it isn't the trout."

"You're right," Evan said. "I'm almost always within earshot of him when we go anywhere. Then again, maybe he thought the woods would cure my moodiness."

Ria looked up at him. Tall, dark-haired, intelligent. A tingle swept over her body, settling in her groin, a warm feeling she'd never had before. Her eyes opened wide. So that's what all the chatter is about! My first crush! *Makes sense. Two months after my first period and now I'm getting urges. Crap! I don't want to wind up like these other women, at the mercy of hormones. But dang! It feels so good!*

"Are you all right, Ria?"

Ria looked up and grinned. "Yeah, I'm fine. Just a flush. I'm sure it will go away." *But do you want it to go away? Dang, dang, double dang!*

"Here they are," Chuck said when he saw them approach. "So, you're Gregory's grandson."

"And Keith and John's son," Evan said, his hand out to shake Chuck's. "But I guess Silas told you that John died two months ago."

"Yes, he did. That was unfortunate." Chuck winced at his choice of words. "Shoot, I'm sorry, losing a parent is so much more than that. I'm sure it was devastating. How's Keith doing?"

"He's grieving. We all are. Even Grandpa Gregory, the ironman of composure, lost it. John wasn't his biological son, but he loved him just as much, maybe even more since he had chosen to be a part of the family, not obligated to be."

"That's a wonderful way to put it," Chuck said. "So, it looks like you and Ria found each other."

Ria blushed unexpectedly at the words 'each other.' Chuck noticed it but didn't react. Instead, he nodded to the stick in Evan's hand. "Looks like I have four fish to fry. I'm glad you caught big ones. It's our last night here and we might as well feast. Too bad you didn't catch the old man."

"I did, but Ria put him back. It was nice seeing him, though. After she told me about him, I sort of felt bad about these," Evan said.

"Don't," Ria said, coming up to touch his elbow in reassurance. "Just think of these fish as carrots in the garden, put there for us to harvest. We just left the old man in his element so he could get bigger. His day will come, but it wasn't today."

"Sounds like you've brought up a philosopher," Silas said. He

86

put out his hand. "I don't think we've ever met," he said, studying her face, so much like Vickie's.

"She looks a lot like the Stillwater's girl, doesn't she?" Evan asked.

"That girl's a Thornwhistle," Silas corrected. "Hal Stillwater and Roger are cousins. They're close, very close." *No need to share the girl's name or tell anyone that they're sisters! Chuck already knows it and Evan doesn't need to.*

Chuck felt the awkwardness in the air and decided a distraction was needed. "Silas, while I get this fish going, would you show Ria around the new RV? You're more familiar with it than I am, anyhow."

"It would be my pleasure." Silas turned sideways, arm stretched out to grandstand the introduction to their new residence and clinic. "Your new castle, Miss."

"It's not new, Ria," Chuck called after them. "It's gently used, but definitely much better than what we've had for the last thirteen years."

"Wow!" Ria went to the sink and marveled at the faucet, touching the spray head appreciably. "And this range! Three burners and an oven, too? What's this?"

"That's a microwave. It runs on electricity, not gas. There's a built-in generator by the back wheel well. It runs on gas, so I guess in a way, the microwave does, too," Silas explained, then looked away, resisting the urge to stare and try to find differences between the two girls. He knew there weren't any, though. They were definitely identical. Two of three.

Ria stepped into the back. "Two bedrooms!" she exclaimed. "You mean, I get my own room? I won't have to sleep on the kitchen bench?"

"That's right," Silas said. "That's one of the requirements your father asked for: privacy for you. As you can see, it's still small, but any bigger and it would be too big to drive into the spots you two seem to be so fond of finding to set up shop."

"Clinic," Ria corrected mindlessly as she looked around the living room. "These chairs will have to go. We can put our old exam table right here, maybe a small desk and two chairs there in the corner. Yes, get rid of the couch and this could be the perfect office and exam room combination." She looked up at Silas. "Did you know I've never been in a traditional doctor's office? One of these days, I'd like to check one out just to see how the rest of the world works."

"When I get my own place, I'll make sure you're one of the first to see it," Evan said.

Silas looked at the youth, then grinned. These were the first words of hope for his future Evan had spoken since his father had fallen ill to cancer. The long ordeal had taken its toll on him, but evidently, there was more than one kind of healing in these backwoods. He noticed the look on Evan's face as he watched for Ria's answer. Oops! He'd have to make sure the boy – young man, he reminded himself – knew that Ria was only thirteen. There was definitely an attraction between the two.

***

"Daddy, I have a question for you," Ria said, pensive but curious. She'd never felt this hesitation before and didn't want to be intimidated by her new emotion.

"You know you can ask me anything," he said, suddenly uneasy at her wariness.

"Did you know that two men could be a couple?"

"Yes, and two women can be, too. Why do you ask?"

"Because Evan said he had two dads but one of them died."

"Yes, I knew both of them before you were born. They were very happily married."

"How come I never knew about it?"

"I never saw a reason to bring it up. You were never going to meet them, as far as I knew. John and Keith, that is. There are loads of same-sex couples, but in these backwoods, most of the people are ultra-conservative. They don't believe that it's possible for two

88

people of the same gender to be compatible, to want to live their lives together as a couple." He looked deep into her eyes. "Every one of us is different. One of these days, you'll start to get urges. I don't know if you'll get them for another woman or a man. It doesn't matter which. As long as you are responsible and don't have sex before you're married, all will be fine."

"So, if I fell in love and wanted to marry another woman, you'd let me?"

"Ria, you can pretty much do anything you want after you're eighteen. I'd prefer that you decided on who you wanted to spend the rest of your life with after you were in your twenties or thirties, though. Before that, urges are mostly hormonal. Strictly chemical with a tad of physical appeal thrown in."

"You mean most people don't fall in love with ugly people?"

"Skin ugly is usually what people see first. After getting to know a person, you'll see the inner beauty. The same goes for someone who is handsome on the outside. They can be horribly ugly inside: mean, vicious, or cruel. Just get to know people before deciding how close you want to be to them. Be nice to others. If they don't treat you the same way, then move on. They don't belong in your life."

"So, you and Friday…" she prompted, hoping he would answer her inferred question.

"I loved Friday very much, but we didn't have that physical attraction. She and Angus did. Now, are we done with this? I need to finish taking what I want from this place. We're heading out early in the morning."

"Yes, sir," she said, using her 'be polite to new people' voice. "I'll be ready in the morning, too."

***

Later that evening

"So, Silas, did you happen to see Vickie when you went to pick up my loan from the Thornwhistles?"

"Yes, I did. We didn't interact, though. She was on her way out the door with her nanny. It's eerie, seeing both girls. They truly are identical. They move alike, have the same sway when they walk, even flip their hair out of their faces in the same manner."

"Have you ever seen the other one, Tori?"

"Nope. Luther and Leanne evidently sold everything they had and headed west. Not that they had much. They were botanists but the patents Luther should have been credited for went to his boss. I would have been bitter about the loss, but he said it had to be a sign that corporate life wasn't for them. I'm not sure where they are, but I can find out if you'd like."

"No, don't bother. I'm sure they'll pop up sometime in the future," Chuck said, an empty spot in his gut screaming for closure. *Just tell him you'd like to see all the girls together one more time. Chicken!* Chuck shook off his insecurities and looked back at Silas. "What about Keith? How's he doing?"

"I'm sure he'd love to see you again, but I think he still has a lot of grieving left to work through. It's been hard on him and Evan. Tonight was the first time I've heard anything positive out of the boy. I know they're not related biologically, but they're similar in so many ways. Keith may be more of a numbers sort of man, but he's also passionate about life and making the most out of it. I see the same trait in Evan. It wouldn't hurt for you to pop into their lives and do a little mentoring for his son."

"Silas, I don't have to hide anything from you. The truth is, I still have feelings for Keith. It's been twenty years since we were together. Whether it was puppy love or not doesn't make a difference. He's like a twenty-dollar chocolate truffle. I know I can't indulge, but the desire is still there."

"Chuck, give it time. Evan was supposed to start pre-med this fall. When John started going downhill fast, both he and Keith put their lives on hold to be with him every minute possible. When he died, Evan spent a lot of time alone. The isolation was tough on Keith, but he knew his son had to grieve in his own way. Seeing you make something out of nothing in this poor section of the world gives the boy a sparkle in his eye I thought wasn't possible."

"Are you sure the sparkle wasn't for Ria?"

Silas chuckled. "Yeah, well there is that attraction. Don't worry. I'll make sure he knows her age. He has a lot of school left before he can go out on his own."

"You said he was starting pre-med in the fall. He couldn't be more than nineteen. How'd he do that?"

"He's eighteen. Like Ria, he's bright. Very bright. He graduated from high school at fourteen, then did five years of college in four. He has a passion for healing that I've only seen twice before."

Chuck grinned. "Don't tell me; Dad and me."

"Okay, I won't tell you, but you're right. By the way, the old man says you owe him about thirteen birthday and Christmas cards. Don't keep away too long. He may be out of the woods when it comes to cancer, but you and I know that it could come back at any time. Even if not, he's not a spring chicken."

"Yeah, he's an old cock and sent you here to give me a heavy dose of guilt for staying away."

"He doesn't need to give you any and neither do I. Anyone with any acuity at all could see you've been beating yourself up for the last decade or so. When are you going to come back and see Grace? You know, don't you, that she doesn't know she had triplets. It was four years before she knew that her 'twins' were even possibly alive. That so-and-so doctor who delivered her told her they died."

"He did? I knew he had told the other two sets of parents that she had died in childbirth and the babies with her, but I didn't know he told Grace they were dead, too. Good God, man. That's horrible! Grace must have thought she was responsible somehow. Shit! I don't need this kind of guilt!"

"You don't need any kind of guilt. You saved the girls and from what I've heard, you also saved that young woman you call Friday. Whatever happened to her?"

"A big, dark-haired Scot came out of the woods and spirited her away. Took her to Scots Dale or someplace in these woods and married her. He said he wanted to give her lots of babies, so I hope that's what happened. If you ever hear from her, let me know, would you?"

"Why would I hear from her?" Silas asked.

"Because I gave her one of your cards. I gave one to her husband, too. Angus McDermott is his name. I didn't know I was going to miss her so much. It's been eight years, but it hurts like it was last week."

"Chuck, I love you like a son," he said, his hand heavy and comforting on his shoulder, "so I'm telling you this. Find someone. Even if it's just dating and casual groping, go out and interact. Make sure the next place you set up your clinic is near enough to civilization that you can go out and have a beer with the guys. At least then if you do come in and reconnect with Keith, you'll know whether it's an old infatuation or the real thing."

Chuck reached up and patted Silas's hand, grateful for the advice. "Thanks, I needed that. I mean, I really didn't need permission, but I did if you know what I mean."

"Absolutely. Come on. Let's go check out the accommodations."

"And chaperone the youngsters," Chuck added.

"Yup," Silas said. "I never reared a daughter, but when they get to this age, it has to be scary."

Chuck looked back at Silas with eyes narrowed. *He didn't say he'd never fathered a daughter. Maybe the rumors were true. Could he really be Grace's sire?* His face relaxed into a smile. *Sire, possibly. But Hal was one-hundred percent Grace's daddy.*

***

"Thanks for showing me how to fish," Evan said, his hand out to shake Ria's.

Instead, she came in and gave him a big hug like she'd seen her father give Silas. *Tingle!* She pulled back and half-smiled, half-grimaced at the new sensation. "I'll find another good fishing spot near wherever it is we're going next. Maybe you can come back."

"I'd like that. How about we have a standing fishing date? As they say, same time next year?"

Ria shrugged, hoping her blush wasn't as red as it felt. "I never heard that phrase, but sure. Silas and Dad keep in contact. I'm sure he'd like to come with you. Maybe your dad would like to come fishing, too? If he hasn't experienced it in a while, it might make him feel better."

Evan nodded, then looked away, the tears starting again. *Dammit!*

"Look, we all have to die. Your father is at peace right now. It's those he left behind who are hurting. I don't know if that makes you feel better or not, but I'm sure he'd want you to move on. Don't forget him, for sure, but find the joy in life. Remember the little things he taught you and share those with others. Did he teach you how to draw or tie fancy knots? How about baking or wood carving? That's what I'm talking about. You're his legacy. Don't let what he taught you in love be lost by not sharing."

"How old are you again?" Evan asked. "I mean, you don't look that old, but you sure have an adult spirit. You're smarter than the counselors I've been talking to for the last three months."

Ria punched him in the upper arm. "Age is just a number. Yup, I'm an old soul. That's what happens when you don't interact with kids your own age when you're growing up."

"Well, kudos to your dad for raising you right."

"I'm not a carrot or a tomato," Ria said with a smirk. "I'm a person. He reared me or brought me up."

"Gotcha," Evan said. He picked up her hand and kissed it gently. "Lady Ria."

She inhaled deeply at the sensation. "Rhianna," she sighed.

"All right then," he said, still holding her hand. He brought it up to his lips again and said, "Farewell, Lady Rhianna. I hope to see you next summer. Next time, I'll bring you a handkerchief."

"Come on, kids," Chuck said. "Break it up. Silas has stuff he needs to do back in the real world, I'm sure."

"Yes, I have 'stuff' to do," Silas said, "but I think *this* is the real world. Where we live is more synthetic. If I had to do it all over again, I'd be rural like you two."

A wide grin spread across Evan's face. "I like that idea. Being a country doctor sounds like a very good plan."

Chuck reached out to shake Evan's hand. "Just make sure you finish school first. You could do it without a degree, but having that doctor's certificate will keep you out of trouble if it ever comes calling. Think of it as having a vaccine. Painful at first, but worth it in the long run to keep the really bad buggers away."

"See you next year, Dr. Armstrong," Evan said, shaking Chuck's hand heartily.

"And say hi to your dad for me," Chuck said. *And thanks for giving me hope, too.*

Chapter 7: Fifteen and Sixteen

Summer, 2006

"I hope you don't think of me as a bad penny that keeps showing up," Evan said.

Ria took the pole out of his hand and unwound the knot that had formed around one of the eyelets. "Bad penny? Nope. I can't even say you're an annoyance. Actually, other than you and Silas, we don't have anyone who keeps popping into our lives. Shoot, we're so mobile, I think that if I've known anyone for more than a year, they're an old acquaintance."

"So, you don't have any family at all?" Evan asked, taking back the pole.

"Just Dad and me."

"Me, too. Sorta," Evan said. His face skewed up, wondering if he should say something or not.

"Okay, what's on your mind," Ria said. "You have that look again…"

"Well, if you're Rhianna Armstrong and your dad is Chuck Armstrong, that means that Papa Doc is your grandfather."

"Who?"

"Papa Doc."

"Papa Doc Duvalier? The Haitian dictator?"

"Ugh! No, Papa Doc Armstrong. He lives up the road from us. I see him at barbecues and get-togethers every once in a while. My dad's been getting out more and more and taking me with him."

"Why do you think we're related?"

"Duh! Come on, Ria. Same last name, same friends, same occupation…"

"Could be a coincidence."

"They look alike, too. I mean, Chuck's a younger version of Papa Doc. I could ask if you'd like."

"Nah, I'll ask my dad when the time is right. He's kind of

sensitive about our isolation and the reasons behind it. I mean, his mission is to take care of people in rural areas without access to health care, but sometimes I think it's just an excuse to stay hidden."

"Do you think he's on the lam or something?"

"Lamb?"

"Lam. It's a term that means he's lying low to keep away from the law."

"Nope. If he was, he wouldn't be using his real name."

"True. Not that you advertise or anything."

"Word of mouth has been working for fifteen years. Why spend money on it?"

"Hey," Evan said, suddenly changing the subject and his attitude. He set the fishing pole on the ground next to the blanket. "I want to take a picture of you. I got this new phone and the camera in it is fantastic."

"A camera in a phone?" Ria strode through the shallow water to where he stood digging into his front pocket.

"Yeah, it's the latest cellphone. It won't work out here for making calls because there aren't any cell towers, but I can still take pictures and notes or do computations on it. It has a calculator and even some games to play if I'm really bored. Actually, the only game I ever play is Solitaire."

"I understood two things: calculator and Solitaire. I have a calculator at home and a deck of cards to play Solitaire. How does that relate to a phone?"

"Haven't you ever seen digital or electronic games?"

"I've seen pinball machines. Is that what you mean?"

"Come over here and let me show you," Evan said, guiding her back to the bank where their blanket was spread out. "One of these days, I'm going to have to get your father to take you to where real civilization is." Seeing the frown on her face, he changed his approach. "There is a whole different world once you get on the grid."

Ria's scowl grew, indignation close and anger only one wrong word away.

"The electrical grid is what folks generally mean, but ninety-five percent of America – or thereabouts – are connected by computers and electronics. One day, there will be free wi-fi for everyone, everywhere, mark my words."

"I know what hi-fi is. Is wi-fi just another form of high fidelity?"

"Actually, it's a trademark name referring to wireless networking connections. Do you have a telephone?"

"No, but I know what one is. If we need one, we go to the library or a market. They almost always have a payphone."

"And those phones are connected to wires which are connected to more wires, right?"

"Yes…"

"Well, this IEEE 802.11x technology uses radio waves to communicate from a base to the unit receiving the waves. In a home network, the router moves the signal from a cell tower or cable to a device such as a computer or a cellphone. This cellphone has little bars that show how strong the signal is."

Ria took the phone and turned it over, checking out the bright blue and white cover and small built-in monitor screen. "I don't see any bars on this."

Evan scooted close to her and leaned in to shade the sun from the device. "Here, it was sleeping." He clicked the button and the screen brightened up to show a river scene with a young Evan and two men, one at either side, all of them smiling. The image was peppered with small icons.

"That's me and my dads when I was thirteen. I'm not very old, but those were the good old days. Those little pictures are shortcut icons to apps."

"I'd say you were speaking Greek, but since I know some Greek, that has to be a whole new language."

"You're close. I was speaking Geek. There are new words coming into the English language every day. Apps is short for applications, but everyone says apps. Technology has become a universal language. People are connected to the internet all over the world. It's unstoppable. Revolutions can be won or lost with information or the lack of it. These little devices are the key. Did you know they even have phones that don't need cell towers – the repeaters? They bounce the signals off of satellites." He pointed to the sky. "Scary, huh?"

"Does that mean those satellites can look down on the user, too?"

"Probably. They have imaging that can read the text on the book a man's reading from its orbit miles above the earth." He thought about what he had just said. "Well, if they don't have that ability today, they will in the next few years. The learning curve of man and artificial intelligence devices is phenomenal. Just think of it as how much faster you started accumulating data after you started reading."

"Accumulating data? That's a weird way to say learn." Ria ran her tongue over her teeth as she realized how ignorant she was of the world. She knew more about the human body and healing than most people, but a simple word such as 'app' was foreign to her. Four-year-olds in ninety-five percent of the world probably knew what it meant!

"Do you think my dad knows about cellphones?"

Evan's face fell. He had said too much. He knew Chuck had a cellphone. It was old technology but still worked. Silas had sent him texts on it in the past. The texts wouldn't show up unless Chuck moved into an area with cell reception, but the two of them had agreed years ago to do that at least once a month. "You'll have to ask Chuck about that," he said, skirting the answer that wasn't his to share.

Ria sighed deeply. The conflict on Evan's face was as plain as the freckles across the bridge of his nose. She wouldn't push it. "So, where's the camera in this thing?" she asked, leaning as close as she dared. She'd like to think she had control over her own body, but it took more effort not to reach out and touch him when he was seated close and without a shirt.

Pushing arrow and enter buttons on the bottom half of the device, Evan opened up several apps and finally the camera. "Would you let me take a picture of you?"

"Yeah, why not?"

"How about going over there and holding up a couple of those fish we caught? You can hold up mine, too, if you'd like."

"Nah. I'll just hold up my big one. Can you make a print copy for my dad? As far as I know, he doesn't have any pictures of me."

Evan's eyes widened but he remained mum. Talk about a private man! He was positively obsessive with his desire to keep himself and his daughter in hiding.

Ria held up the twelve-inch-long trout up and smiled.

Snap! Snap!

"Now, make a silly face. This one's for me."

Holding the fish so she was face-to-face with it, Rhianna pretended to kiss it.

"Perfect! Now, put it back with the others then step away. I want your whole body in this shot."

"Why?"

"Because when I come back next year, I want you to see how much you've changed. I wish I had taken a picture of you the first day we met. You were a cutie then, but nothing like you are now. I can't wait to see what you look like when you're fully grown."

"Well, I have to say that sounds sexist and condescending and a few other negative adjectives!" said in a harsh tone.

"No, no! That's not what I meant," Evan answered. "Do you want to take a picture of me? I'm sure I've changed a lot since we first met, too."

"Stand up and turn around," Ria said, her tone still chilly.

"I really didn't mean to offend you," he said softly, obeying her instructions, slowly turning in place. "I'd never intentionally say or do anything to upset you or embarrass you or…"

"Hold it right there," Ria said, cutting off his groveling. "You look like you've added more muscle mass. Have you been working out?"

His back to her, he looked over his shoulder and said, "I'm on the rowing team in school. I know I had to buy larger shirts. I also grew an inch and a half in the last year. I guess I'm a late bloomer."

"Yeah, well, as my daddy always says, perfection takes time."

Evan's face reddened. He cleared his throat and turned to face her. "So, do you think I'm perfect?"

"Nope, but you're getting there."

"My turn," Evan said. "Let me check you out. I mean, I just finished a class in whole body diagnostics. Let me see if I can spot something wrong that even you don't know about."

"Okay…" Ria said hesitantly. "What do you want me to do?"

"Turn away from me."

"Shirt on or off?" she asked.

"Off. I mean, it has to be off so I can see your spine."

Ria yanked her tee-shirt off over her head and tossed it onto the blanket. Last year's bathing suit top barely covered her perky breasts that had grown two sizes in the last year, but she knew she was still decent. "What now?"

You're a doctor, you're a doctor. Look at her with the eyes of an old man looking for defects. Evan touched the tops of both her shoulders at the same time, checking for similarity in muscle tone and height. Then he gently prodded her spine, causing her to giggle and squirm when he got near her waist and above her cutoff jeans. "Arms out straight like you're making a tee."

Ria obeyed, then waited patiently as he tried to lower her arms. "Resist me," he said.

"Every chance I get," she said, then laughed.

"Bend over at the waist," he directed, still standing behind her.

Ria formed a perfect right angle.

"All right. Stand up straight and look at me."

Ria gracefully pivoted in place and looked at him, then changed her focus from his dreamy blue eyes to the end of his nose. "Like this?"

"Shut your eyes, then arms out again and touch your right index finger to your nose. All right, left index finger to nose."

"How much longer? I want to go swimming. It's getting hot."

"Just a couple more. Stand on one foot. Now the other. Shoot! I can't remember the rest of the poses. Yes, Ria, you're pretty much perfect. At least, you're coordinated and perfectly symmetrical."

"Done then?"

"Yeah, sure."

Her back still to him, she picked her way to the edge of the deep pool. "Too early for fishing," she said over her shoulder, then dove in, hiding her embarrassment at being intimately examined beneath the chilly water.

Evan set the phone down, kicked off his tennis shoes, and followed suit, coming up out of the water right next to her. "I don't ever want to fight with you or offend you. I know we're too young for anything serious, but you really are my best friend. I mean, I have lots of acquaintances in school and through the country club, but I never share anything deep with them. Like how I felt about the loss of my dad and such. You're the only one who knows the real me."

"But we only write letters and see each other once a year for a few days."

"Ria, do you realize how special you are? I have to respect the fact that you've been isolated and kept from the world as I know it. When I show you parts of it, though, you pick up on everything so quickly. You're bright and kind and everything a man could want as a partner or best friend."

"Except I'm too young…"

"Yeah, well, I'm definitely going to respect that! I don't know who would castrate me first if I did anything to compromise your virtue: Silas or your dad. I'm not going to find out, though. I never knew I was a patient man, but I'm finding out that I am. But, we both have a lot of growing to do and knowing that helps with restraint."

"How's school going?" Ria asked, her head bowed, very uncomfortable with the direction their conversation was going, especially since he was standing in the pool so close to her, his bare chest next to her barely covered one.

Evan reached over and brought her chin up so she was looking at him. She was only a scant foot away, definitely in the danger zone if he couldn't control his urges. "I'm doing everything I can to graduate early. Everything, that is, except take summer classes that would interfere with the little bit of time we have together. Silas's excuse for bringing me along on his annual checkups is that he's grooming me to take over for him when he dies. He says he's not that old, but death can snatch a person away in his prime. That happened to my dad and almost happened to Papa Doc. He wants to make sure there's someone he trusts to keep the secrets."

"What kind of secrets?" Ria asked, a mischievous grin on her once dour face.

"Ahh... If I told you that, what kind of secret keeper would I be?" he answered. "The one secret I will share with you is one of my own. I want to move away from traditional healing. I only have a year to go for my MD degree, but I plan on taking classes on holistic medicine."

"Whole-body healing?" Ria asked, although she already knew the answer.

"You say that as if you know all about it."

"I do. That's pretty much what Daddy does. He never calls it that, though. I found out when I was doing my own studying. We don't accumulate much, but I don't think he's ever thrown away a medical book. It might be a hassle finding the right one since a lot of the older ones are in boxes that we use to support the mattresses, but unless it's an old PDR, he keeps it."

"PDR?"

"You mean I know something you don't? It's Physicians' Desk

Reference."

"I know what you mean, but I have mine on my phone. I'll show you when we get out."

"I never thought about having books on an electronic device. I know the library has a computer, but I never really investigated how to use one. I just check out as many books as I can carry and leave."

"Just like learning to read, once you master computers and the internet, a whole new world opens up to you. I'll see what I can do for you. I might be back before next year. After all, isn't your sweet sixteen birthday coming up?"

"I don't know how sweet it will be, but yes, nine days after Christmas I'll be sixteen."

Evan closed his eyes, trying to think of how he could put together a computer and a receiver for internet that would work in this area. "What are the chances you two will be moving in the next six months?"

"Actually, pretty good. Clients have been slowing down. I think we've fixed up pre-existing conditions – or at least provided long term care plans – for those who have decided to give us a shot. The other ailments are taken care of by the volunteer fire department. They hold their own clinic on Sundays in the back room of the post office. It's quaint, but they'll actually come out to the folks if stitches are needed."

"I take it that service wasn't available before you and your dad came here."

"Yeah, it was my suggestion. They ate it up. Sometimes folks can't see that they have their own solutions to problems because they're too close to them. It takes an outsider to point them out."

"And that's another thing I love about you," Evan said, then blushed scarlet at his admission of attraction.

Ria grinned at his discomfort. "I think it's time to get out of the water. We're going to be all pruney."

"I'll let you get out first," Evan said. "I think I'll take a lap." *Take a lap or three and try to hope the excitement goes down!*

Damned body won't listen to reason or the fact that you're only fifteen!

Ria swam to the edge of the deep pool then stepped out, being careful of the slippery rocks. She had built a series of steps this spring, as soon as the water was warm enough, but they were already grown over with moss. She teetered on one and reached out, trying to stay upright. Grabbing air and losing her balance, she gave up her awkward struggle and fell backward, into the cushion of the water.

Seeing her distress, Evan had rushed forward, ready to catch her if she fell, waiting for her with open arms. "Watch your head!" he shouted as she dropped.

Splash!

Turning sideways to avoid clunking heads, Evan brought his hand up and lifted her shoulders out of the water. "Are you all right?" he asked.

"Just about three shades of embarrassed is all."

"Don't worry. I got your back. Always."

"I know you do. Come on. Help me out. I won't look. I'll even throw you a towel."

Now it was Evan's turn to blush. "I guess you're not as young as I thought."

"I am, but remember, I've been in the rough and tumble world of folks who don't hold back on their explanations of life and what's going on. I've never watched a soap opera, but I'm sure I've seen the storyline of most of them."

Gently touching her back in reassurance as they both walked up the slippery steps together, Evan looked down to make sure things had calmed down with fear. They had, but with touching her, he was getting hard again. He pulled his hand away and a chilly breeze came up at the same time. *Phew! A natural remedy!*

"Here. I think we should head back. My body thinks it's older than it is. If I hang out here too much longer, my brain will lose its veto vote."

"Gotcha," Evan said, taking the towel from her. "As long as one of us keeps a cool head, we'll be okay. Heaven help us if we both lose control."

***

December 27th, 2007
One week before Ria's 16th birthday

"You got another letter from Evan," Chuck said, handing her an oversized card envelope. "This one feels like it's another picture. You did tell him thanks for this one, didn't you?" he asked, nodding to the five-by-seven acrylic framed photo of her holding a big trout that graced his desk.

"Yes, I did," she said absent-mindedly, rushing to open the first letter she'd had in a month.

Dear Ria,

I'm sorry I haven't written as much lately. I'm in clinicals now and have been running on four to five hours of sleep a night. I wish I could be there for your sixteenth birthday but I can't seem to squeeze even eight hours to myself much less the two days of travel it would take to just see you for a few moments.

I was downloading everything off my old phone onto my new one when I found this. It was saved to the wrong folder. Actually, it popped up just when I needed it most, so I guess it wasn't the 'wrong' folder after all. I printed it out and have it on my desk and in my wallet. It even pops up on my screensaver. You're always just a smile away from me.

Ask your father to give you a big hug from me. If all goes well, I should be able to come out at spring break.

Warmest regards,

Evan

"What did you get?" Chuck asked.

"Looks like a picture," Ria said, tearing off the paper toweling wrapped around the acrylic frame.

"Oh, my God! I totally forgot about this! Look!"

Ria handed her father the photo of her 'kissing' the trout.

105

"Oh, is there any way you'll let me put this on my desk?" he asked.

"Nope. This is coming into my room. I don't need any smart-aleck remarks coming from our clients. These folks don't know it was a joke. They already think I'm weird. They might believe I really was kissing the fish! Besides, if this is what brightens his day, just seeing it and knowing he's looking at the same image, maybe at the same time, means a lot to me."

"You are such a romantic, Ria. Where'd you get that from?" Chuck asked, then realized what he had said.

"Must come from that woman who birthed me, eh?" she replied. "Don't worry about it. Good or evil, if there's a trait I have that I don't share with you, I'll always credit or blame it on her. Believe it or not, I never felt deprived. You've done a great job, Mama Daddy."

"You haven't called me that since you were six."

"At least, not out loud or to your face. I'm sorry if I haven't said it enough, but you really are the greatest."

"Yeah, well, Lord knows I tried. But I've often wondered if I didn't do you a disservice by helping you achieve so much of your potential. I've never heard of a sixteen-year-old doctor, but you really do have that magic touch. Plus, you have more skills than many who are out there practicing."

"And that's the reason: practice. I've been practicing for at least ten years."

"I'll never forget you begging me to let you put stitches in that puppy the boar had gored. I thought that old man was going to flip when I said yes. I told him someone had to hold the dog down. I mean, yes, he was a puppy, but he was still at least twenty pounds. Since he wasn't willing…"

"Yup. I really wanted to keep that dog, too."

"That's another thing I regret: never letting you have pets."

"Don't worry about it. We had chickens, didn't we? Besides, I still have a lot of years left to own a dog or cat. However, next time someone offers a nanny goat, I'd appreciate it if you said yes. Goat milk is so much better than canned milk."

"Deal," Chuck said, his hand out.

"Deal!" Ria said, then gave him a big hug. "Now, I have to go find the right place for this. Why I never thought of taking a picture of Evan, I'll never know."

"Because you don't think technology, you think biology."

"Now *that* I get from you!"

***

January 4, 2008 (a week later)

Ria stepped out of the hot shower and dried off quickly. She hastily threw on her sweats and wrapped her hair in a towel. The winter chill in Connecticut was almost impossible to get rid of, but she'd try. She sniffed the air. Breakfast!

"That bacon smells so good," she called out from the hallway. She stepped into the combination exam room and office and saw her father had company. "Oh, I'm sorry, Dad. I didn't know you had clients this early."

"*Who* are you?" the young woman asked.

"Shit! I mean, shoot! Who are *you*?" Rhianna looked at her father. *Who is this person who looks so much like me?* His eyes were wide and mouth still agape. "Daddy? Do I have a twin?"

"Sorta," he said softly, then took a deep breath and shut his mouth. "And yes, saying shit is appropriate in this case."

"So, who's Ria?" the young man asked, intently watching her father for signs of lying.

"I am," Ria answered. "Rhianna Lynn Strong."

Ria flushed as she stammered the last name she and her father had decided to use this far north. She was lying but hoped neither of these two strangers noticed her flub or cared what her last name was.

"So, if she's Rhianna Lynn, and I'm Vickie Lynn, who is Tori Lynn?" the thin young woman who looked so much like her asked.

Chuck took another deep breath and shook his head. "Me and my big mouth. Shoot."

"No, Daddy," Ria said. "Now's an appropriate time to say shit."

"Shit, shoot, either way, that's why I said sorta. You aren't twins – you're two of triplets. You were all adopted when you were just a few hours old to different parents."

Ria and Vickie stared at each other for a moment, then both looked at Chuck. "So, where's our sister?" the one named Vickie asked.

"And who's our mother?" Ria echoed with the exact same tone and inflection.

"Eerie," the young man said.

"Yeah, right?" added Chuck.

"That's an evasive reply," Ria said. "I'm calling you out on that, as you so often say to me."

"Yeah, I guess I brought you up right."

"Yes, you did. And that's another evasive answer," Ria said, hands on hips.

"Are Grace and Dusty our parents?" Vickie asked.

"You know them?" Chuck asked.

"That's answering a question with a question," Vickie said. "Yes, Gloria and Roger brought me up right, too," she said, nudging her new-found sister with an elbow of camaraderie.

"Oh, Lord. I knew this day was coming…"

"Hey, Doc. That's more evasiveness. My parents brought me up right, too," the young man said. "Just don't tell me I'm related to them, okay?"

"Unless Dusty and Grace are your parents, no, you're not related." Doc ran his fingers through his long salt and pepper hair. "Why are you here?"

Vickie turned to the man. "Yeah, why are *you* here, Rich? And you never did have a 'guy problem,' did you?"

"You're the only guy problem I have," he said. "While you three reconnect, can I go to my truck and get some sleep? I've been driving all night after a full day of family and birthday parties and rescuing damsels in distress and… I just need an hour or two.

108

Please?"

"Ria, show Rich to the back bedroom and give him an extra blanket. I don't want him passing out. He's too big for me to move around."

"You've moved bigger," Ria said.

"Not without hurting for the next three days," he replied.

"Just saying…"

"Do you two always talk like that?" Vickie asked Chuck.

"Like what?"

"I don't know. Like she's your wife. You're not weird like that, I hope."

"Ew! No!" Chuck said in disgust. "She's my helper here at the clinic. This place isn't much, but it's all we can afford with how much we charge. We don't take insurance, don't have any foundations funding us, and part of my mission is to be mobile. I'm all over the place in this thing. I fix people up, and then I'm on my way."

"Like in Wolf Whistle?" Vickie asked.

"Do you know why they called it that?" Ria barely paused before answering her own question. "It's because the wind blows so hard, it sounds like it's whistling when it blows through the trees and rocks."

"And cracks in the door and window seals," Chuck added. "We left there years ago. How do you know about that?"

"I found an old money order made out to my mother," Vickie said. "What was that all about?"

"She loaned me money. I paid it back. I called that old motorhome we had The Whistler because it was so drafty. Her loan helped me buy this one. It was used but in much better shape and ten feet longer than the previous one. It's not as negotiable in the hills, but we manage to find a place big enough to park for a month. The little towns and hollows are happy to have us around to treat those who need it. We stay put until clients stop showing up."

"So, does that mean Rhianna's homeschooled?"

"You can call me Ria. Yes, I'm homeschooled. Can I ask you a question? Oh, I just did, didn't I? Oops. Another question. What I'm getting at is, are you sick?"

"No," Vickie replied, embarrassed at someone telling her she was inadequate.

"Hey, Dad. Let me take this one. Go finish your coffee and breakfast. I'm giving this beautiful young lady a check-up. Something's wrong with her and she doesn't even know it."

"But…but…we just met!"

"It's either me or Dad, but one of us is going to find out what's going on in that skinny pasty body. You forget: he and I both know what you *should* look like."

"She's got you there," Chuck said. "She sees herself in the mirror every morning. You may be beautiful, but I agree: you don't look right."

"We're not going back where Rich is, are we?"

"Nope." Ria ushered her to the tiny room on the other side of the office living room combination. "This is my bedroom." She pulled down a cabinet door and revealed a bin of personal belongings, including a pink stuffed unicorn.

Vickie reached up and touched it. "An ooni-corn! I had one almost like it. I was obsessed with them when I was little."

"Really? Me, too!" Ria pulled the animal out and gave it to her. "Hold onto her while I check you out. First, take off your shirt."

"Can I leave on my bra?"

"As long as I don't see anything suspicious, sure. This place is still chilly, even if it isn't as drafty."

Jacket and tee-shirt off, Vickie crossed her arms across her chest and shivered, her bony shoulder bones sharp and angular.

"Geez, woman! You're not much more than a skeleton! Don't your parents feed you?"

"Yeah, they noticed, if that's what you mean. My nanny says I'm too fat. She's bony and thinks I should be, too. If I eat, she makes my life miserable. I swear she has cameras hidden

110

everywhere. If I so much as sneak an olive, she lectures me for an hour on how I'll never get a husband, that fat people have no self-control…"

"Have you told your parents about her?"

Vickie shook her head. "I can't."

"Or won't… So, let me approach this another way. What's the worst that can happen if they fire her?"

"She's already blackmailing them. I just found that out yesterday. Or was that earlier this morning? Anyhow, after my birthday party…" Vickie paused, her eyes glistening in recall of Grace punching Elsa.

"What's wrong? Or what's right?" Ria asked. "Now I know what Dad sees when something's going through my head. What you're feeling is showing on your face."

"Oh, it's right, very right." Vickie grabbed the rainbow afghan from the bed and wrapped it around her shoulders. "Okay, so here's the thing. I was about four when I first met my real mother – our birth mother – but I didn't know who she was. I was never told I was adopted. Everything led me to believe that I was just a late-in-life child. So, one day I kinda got rescued by a woman whose father is my father's – adopted father's – cousin. One thing leads to another, and we're in each other's lives. I sort of get a set of godparents.

"I started suspecting there might be more of a connection when I was thirteen. I confronted Grace – our mom – and she admitted a truth. Not the complete truth, but something she thought would satisfy me. She told me that her mother and my mom – the woman who brought me up – were sisters. None of them got along, so they just ignored each other. That was also her reason why we looked so much alike.

"I didn't get a clue that we were even more closely related until Grace – Mom – punched out Nanny Elsa at my birthday party. She got all wound up when she was slugging it out and referred to me as her daughter. Afterward, she said it was because I was her goddaughter. She tried throwing in a few other smoke and mirrors remarks, but I saw through them. Plus, I saw the shock in her face when she realized that she had claimed me out loud."

"Before I get all distracted with *Mom...*" Ria inhaled deeply with the word, savoring it, then licked her lips, determined not to get distracted. "Why did Mom punch your nanny? I assume Nanny Elsa is your nanny."

Vickie turned her head and showed her the ear that was still itching and burning. "Elsa talked me into getting my ears clipped. This one got infected."

"Ooh. That looks painful. I noticed the difference when I first saw you. I think I should have Dad check that out. So, lie back real quick and let me poke and prod. I think you look so pasty because you're malnourished and fighting an infection."

"Do you know how weird this is?" Vickie asked. "You look and sound just like me. You're not a phantom or a dream." She reached up and touched her arm. "So weird."

"Yeah, I do know, because I get the same feeling. Dad never told me, either." Ria's fingers deftly felt for an enlarged liver or other abnormalities, then satisfied she was in good health, offered her a hand to sit up.

"Yeah... And there's another one of us out there somewhere..." Vickie said dreamily.

"Yeah..." Ria echoed. "Really weird."

"Can I get dressed now?"

"Sure. Hey, let me give you a tank top to wear under everything else. Keeping clothing right next to your skin helps insulate your body heat. After you're dressed, I want Dad to look at that ear."

"Gotcha. Sis."

"Back at ya. Sis."

Both girls shivered in excitement with identical shoulder shrugs, then laughed the same short, "Hah!"

"This is going to be so much fun!" they said at the same time.

I have a sister and a mother and another father! And another sister! So alone in family one minute, and then overloaded with them the next! Sing hallelujah!

Chuck inhaled deeply at seeing the infected wound, resisting the urge to comment on the sloppy work. He stood in front of her and asked, "Have you seen anyone else about this. Other than the person who did the deed?"

"Yeah, Papa Doc cleaned it up last night. He didn't have any lidocaine so let me have a drink of whisky to help numb the pain. How can anyone drink that stuff?"

"They drink it for effect, not flavor. Or so they tell me. Who is this Papa Doc fellow?"

"He's kind of like a grandpa to me. A. B. C. Armstrong is his name. Actually, I have lots of surrogate grandpas. Hal and Silas claim me, too."

So, Silas knows about me having a twin – or rather, two triplet sisters? Does Evan know? Shit! That's what he was talking about the first time he ever saw me. That's why he thought I knew him.

Ria watched and listened rather than join the conversation. Her sister paused her cheery rambling for a moment, then spoke sincerely. "Hey, Chuck. How come you just paled when I said his name?" Vickie looked at her and saw a similar reaction. "Okay, you two. Do you know Papa Doc?"

"He does, I never met him," Ria said. "He won't let me. Papa Doc is his father."

"Oh…" Vickie said, then giggled as realization hit. "You sign reads C. R. M. Strong. That's for Chuck Ar-m-strong, am I right?"

"Turn around and let me clean that ear again," Chuck grumbled, then smiled at her cleverness.

"Oh, my God!" Vickie squealed, bouncing up and down in place.

"Hold still," Chuck ordered, his hand firm on her shoulder. "Which epiphany did you just have?"

"Hal is my grandpa! My honest to goodness biological grandpa. And yours, too, Ria!"

"Took you long enough," Chuck said with a chuckle. "When I'm done, I need to put more topical antibiotics on that. I don't have any antibiotic pills left, so I want you to go back home and tell Papa Doc that your physician in Woodstock said he had confidence that he'll know which one to administer."

"I'm jealous," Ria said with a pout.

"Of what?" Chuck asked.

"She gets to know my grandpa and I don't."

"Both adopted and biological grandpas. And our father and mother..." Vickie said softly.

"Well, meeting them would be cool, too," Ria said. "I never felt shorted when it came to the parents' aspect of a relationship, but I knew about Papa Doc. I never had a grandfather. Dad, can we go there for a visit? I want to meet him."

"We'll see..."

Ria rolled her eyes at her sister and scowled. *That means no.* A grin bloomed and she raised an eyebrow. *But I have you now. Will you help?*

Face pinched in discomfort as the swab cleaned out the wound, Vickie cut her eyes to the side and gave a discreet thumbs-up. *I got your back, Sis!*

Chapter 8: Eighteen and Legal

January 28, 2010

"I had to call in a lot of favors," Evan said, "but I have forty-eight hours off. I couldn't swing the wedding, though. Can you text me the address of the rehearsal dinner? I should be able to make it by seven."

"Sure. Hey, would you help me play a trick on my dad?"

"You name it! He's been making me squirm for the past five years. Just make it a good one. I'll probably only get one shot."

"Okay. I have Vickie's wedding dress with me. We can't do it at the rehearsal tonight, but we can do it tomorrow. We'll have to build up to it at dinner, though, dropping subtle hints that should drive him nuts."

"What are you talking about?"

"I'm going to come out wearing Vickie's wedding dress! I think tomorrow at noon ought to do it. We can make sure everyone but him knows about it, making him think he's being left out of our wedding on purpose."

"Isn't that a little too mean?" Evan asked. "I don't mind making him feel uncomfortable, but I don't want to gut the poor guy."

"Nah, he'll be fine. Maybe I won't tell anyone else. That way he won't feel too singled out."

"Speaking of single, what's going on between our two dads? They sure have been in close contact for the last few months. Not that I'm complaining. Dad is finally through the miserable part of grieving. I know he still misses Father, but at least he isn't crying anymore. Well, not that I've seen. Actually, he has a spring to his step that I don't remember *ever* seeing."

"Oh, my God! Do you think they're dating?" Ria asked, her hands under her chin with excitement.

A series of emotions raced across Evan's face as he considered the implications. He shook his head, trying not to think of them.

"Ria, I have to ask you something right now. It's actually pretty time-sensitive."

"Sure, what gives?" she asked, not giving him her complete attention, thinking instead of all the hints and suggestions she'd drop to make her father squirm at the thought of her getting married.

"You didn't hear me, did you?" Evan asked.

"I'm sorry," Ria said. "You're right. My mind is all over the place right now. Go ahead. I know you said it was time-sensitive and here I go, fantasizing about a make-believe wedding."

"Would you marry me? We don't have to do it right away, the wedding that is, or anything else. I mean," he stammered. "I'm not asking just to keep up with your sister and Rich. I do want you to be my wife – or at least my fiancée – before my dad and your dad get too serious, though. I don't want to marry my stepsister, but do want to marry you. Actually, I've wanted to marry you since…"

"Yes! Yes! Yes!" Ria exclaimed, jumping up into his arms. She smothered him with excited kisses, then bent down for a long and thorough smooch that sent tingles throughout. She finally pulled back. "You've wanted to marry me since when?"

"Since you were fifteen and a half, I think. That sounds so perverted, especially since I was twenty, but it was only your body that was young."

"No, my body and my social skills were both juvenile. Intellectually, I was an adult, but I had to have a lot of life experiences in a short time to get to where I am today. Spending weekends with Vickie and Gloria, Papa Doc and Silas helped. It was good for my dad, too, having time away from me. But I often felt like something was missing in my life. Even finally meeting Grace and Dusty and acknowledging them as my bio-parents didn't fill that void. No, I never felt complete until we were together for our few days every summer. When you were gone, it was as if I was pinging a signal and no one was there to acknowledge it. You stepped back into my life and –voila! – the signals and circuits were completed."

"So, you'll wear the dress for a preview? It won't be just to

116

punk him?"

"Let's just say we're going to prepare him. I'm sure Vickie will let me borrow her dress when she's done with it. I do want to wait until you're done with internships or residencies or whatever comes next before getting married. From what I've heard, they run you ragged those last few months. You don't need to worry about taking care of your wife at the same time."

"Honey, taking care of you is going to be a pleasure." Evan reached down and readjusted himself through his slacks. "And if part of me had its way, it'd be pleasuring you right now!"

"Well, we are betrothed…" Ria cooed.

Knock! Knock! Knock!

"Hey! Are you in there, Ria?" Vickie called.

"Damn!" Ria hissed. "Yeah, I'll be right out!" she hollered.

"To be continued?" Evan asked.

"I certainly hope so. But remember, dress up nice tomorrow so you'll be ready for the show at noon."

Vickie paced the hall in front of the room her sister had sneaked into, waiting impatiently for her to answer. The door opened a crack, then Ria slipped out, a tall dark-haired man following very close behind her. Both had flushed faces tinged with embarrassment. No need to call them out on what they'd been doing!

"Hey, Sis," Vickie said. "I sort of need a favor. Could you cover for me for an hour or so at dinner?"

"What? You're going to miss your own rehearsal dinner?" Ria asked, then felt the loss of Evan. She turned and watched as he ducked into the men's room.

"No, I'm just going to be late," Vickie said, her face reddening.

"You know, you're a lousy liar," Ria said. "Tell me what's going on, or at least enough that I can give a believable excuse. You do know I'm supposed to be there, too."

"Yeah, I know. This gets a little sticky. I don't want anyone to get in trouble, but Rich is in a bind. I have to sort of bail him out. Not bail as in he got arrested, but as in a predicament. Just be me for a few minutes, make an excuse for Rich, then duck out and come back in as yourself. It'll be believable if your hair's down."

"Okay, but I want to ask a favor. Can I borrow your dress tomorrow? You won't need it until Saturday. I want to wear it to shock the stuffing out of my dad."

"Why?"

"Why not? I'm sorry. That sounded cruel. I think it's because I have eighteen years of childish pranks backed up in me. I never got to do this kind of stuff when I was young. I don't know if it's stress or excitement or jealousy or whatever because you're getting married first, but I suppose just once I want to see my 'always mellow and in control' dad wound up about something!"

"Sure. It's at the house hanging outside my closet. You know the access code to get in. If that makes you feel uncomfortable, just ring the bell. You know you're always welcome. Of course, if you need to get rid of some more of that mischief, go ahead and pretend you're me. Just let me know what you're doing and when, so I don't meet myself coming or going!"

"Thanks," Ria said and gave Vickie a quick kiss on the cheek. "You're the best."

"Back at ya," Vickie said, then left to rescue Rich from his fraternity brothers' bachelor party.

Ria waited until she was sure her sister was gone, then knocked on the men's room door. "Coast is clear," she said.

Evan came out, his face and hair damp.

"What happened to you?" she asked.

"I couldn't take a cold shower, so I did the next best thing: stuck my head in the sink under cold running water. Are you sure you want to wait until I'm done with my internship?"

"Come on. I have to play Vickie's role at her own wedding rehearsal dinner. You'll have to wait in the wings until I leave. Then we can come back in as ourselves. It's a small price to pay for borrowing the wedding dress. I'm sure she would lend it to me anyway, but this is going to be my grandest performance. All the parents and grandparents will be there."

"You didn't answer my question," Evan said, nudging her shoulder.

"I have a plan about that," Ria said, a twinkle in her eye. "I've been reading books that aren't on my dad's approved reading list. I have a plan for your – shall we say? – discomfort? Don't ask. Let me surprise you after we get pretend married tomorrow. I hear it's the next best thing and won't get me pregnant."

"Man, I'm glad you're eighteen now!" Evan exclaimed in a hushed voice. "Just tell me where you want me and when. I'm yours to command, fiancée!"

***

"I can't do it," Ria said. "I can't go out there and fool everyone who loves her. It's not fair to them."

"Then don't do it," Evan said. "Teasing someone is one thing, but truly pretending to be someone you're not isn't right."

"Okay. I got a plan. Hang back in the foyer until I call for you, all right?"

"Your wish is my command," Evan said. He looked at his watch. "At least for the next eighteen hours or so."

Ria waited until the wedding party had settled down at their tables and were looking everywhere for the bride and groom to be. "It's time," she whispered to herself.

Entering the room to an audience of friends and family, all standing up and cheering the person they thought was Vickie, Ria waved to the group and threw kisses. "Thank you, thank you, thank you," she said, then walked up to her place at the center of the long table of honor. She stood next to the empty chair where Rich should have been and put her hand on the back, waiting for the crowd to settle down.

"I'm sure many of you also came here to see Rich." She nodded to Rick Rickman, Rich's father, then the woman at his side, Mrs. Rickman. "Well, unfortunately, young Mr. Rickman has been detained. And if you haven't figured it out already, his dear fiancée

119

has rushed to his side to take care of his dilemma."

The low rumble of whispers covered the room like a soft blanket. "Yup, it's me: Rhianna. Vickie asks your indulgence in not being able to be here, but I can understand her choice. Great food and good company over the health and security of her fiancé. Here, here, to Vickie Lynn Thornwhistle and Rich Rickman!" she said, lifting her glass of sparkling cider.

After the cheers and applause died down, Ria moved toward the mic again. "I'd like to take this opportunity to say a few kind words about my sister, and then invite others to do the same. It's a little unconventional, but so are they." She paused at the silence that followed, then added, "But in a good way," then scurried over to sit next to Gloria, Vickie's mother.

More applause followed, along with the clanging on his glass by Rick Rickman. "I love this family!" he declared, causing more applause. "Has anyone ever seen such flexibility when it comes to unexpected or adverse situations?" More applause.

Gloria leaned over and whispered, "You did great, dear. If your father was here, I'm sure he'd be just as proud of you as we are."

Ria looked up and saw Evan waiting for her signal. She motioned to him, then looked everywhere. No father. What in the heck was this? No bride or groom? Hopefully, the food was good and Vickie and Rich were safe.

Evan sneaked in, hunched over as he approached her side. She nodded to Rich's empty chair beside her. "Might as well be the groom-in-waiting for a while," she whispered. "This is going to be a long night."

***

"Hey, Dad," Ria called out from her bedroom. "How flexible is your schedule today?"

"I don't have any clients lined up, if that's what you mean. No paperwork or chores. No dirty dishes to wash since we ate out, and no dinner to cook, either, because they loaded me up with leftovers. Why? What's on your mind."

Knock! Knock! Knock!

Sweat poured off Evan's forehead despite the winter chill and his lack of warm coat. The tuxedo provided minimal warmth but nerves took care of the rest.

"Evan?" Chuck asked, seeing him dressed up. "Why the tux? The wedding's not until tomorrow."

"Vickie's wedding is tomorrow," Ria said, coming out of her bedroom wearing Vickie's gown, her hair piled in curls atop her head, her eyes blinking at the irritation of wearing mascara for the first time. "I figured today was a good time for ours. Silas is nearby, just waiting to do the honors. What do you say, Daddy? Are you ready to give me away?"

Chuck plopped down on the exam table, his legs as limp as maple syrup dripping off a pancake. "Whoa! When did this happen? You don't *have* to get married, do you?"

"Well, I figured one of us should get married. You didn't and still had a child."

"That's different."

"Daddy, you didn't raise an idiot. I know that babies and marriage don't necessarily go hand in hand. I just thought it would be fun to wear a wedding dress. Did I scare you?"

"Yes," Chuck said, then turned around and looked at the back of his pants. "Oh, thank God." He picked up the cleaning cloth he had left on the exam table and tossed it to the kitchen sink. "I thought I'd shit myself."

"Oh, Daddy," Ria said, rushing up to hug him, her eyes streaming with black mascara. "I thought this would be funny." She paused and allowed herself to chuckle, then looked at Evan to see his reaction. He was ghostly white in fear.

"I guess it wasn't as funny as I thought it'd be. But you do know I'm going to get married one of these days."

"Yeah, well, let me get used to it gradually. Vickie and Rick have been going together for two years. It really wasn't too unexpected."

"Begging your pardon," Evan said, his color returning. "But even if it wasn't dating or 'going together,' Rhianna and I have been fond of each other for five years. I guess what I'm saying is, I've asked Ria to marry me."

"And…" Chuck said, his eyes wide as he looked to Ria.

"And I said, 'Yes!'" Ria exclaimed, jumping up and down. "Oops," she said, then grabbed a tissue from the box on the desk and wiped her eyes. "I can't get the dress dirty. Vickie needs it tomorrow."

"Well, as long as you don't 'need' it tomorrow or anytime soon, that's fine with me. Evan, you're a fine young man, and I appreciate your devotion to my daughter, but don't you think she's a little young to get married?"

"No, I don't or I wouldn't have asked her. I did ask that we wait until I'm done with my internship, but right now, that hasn't been decided."

"How much longer?" Chuck asked. He looked at Ria and saw her blanch. "And would they let you intern at a rural clinic?"

"Oh, Daddy!" Ria exclaimed, her tears sprouting again. "Excuse me, guys. I really have to change out of this dress. I'm so excited, I could pop!"

"Six months, sir. That would make it early summer completion."

"Well, if it makes a difference, put my name down. You might want to ask Papa Doc, too. He has an inner-city clinic that could always use a hand. Between the two of us, we should have your options covered."

***

January 30, the next evening

"So, why were you late to your own rehearsal. Were you and Rich finally getting it on?"

"Ria!" Vickie exclaimed.

"Ah, that's an evasive reply. I'll take that as a yes. Watch it. Grace said she got pregnant the first time."

Vickie blushed, lips pursed in frustration, wanting to deny what her sister suspected but knowing it was no use. She blew out her held breath. "Don't tell anyone, please."

"Duh! It's nobody's business, including mine. Two days early is close enough. You still deserve to wear white."

"What about you, Ria? The hunk? Are you two 'getting it on'?"

"Eet!" Ria made a noise like a penalty buzzer. "Not your business!"

"So, you're not blushing or mad at me for suggesting it which means you're not doing anything, but you'd like to be. I know I've never met him, but he looks familiar."

"Don't concern yourself with us. You're the one getting married in," Ria looked up at the clock, "fifteen minutes. Where are the moms?" she asked, walking to the doorway to look down the hall.

"Oooh! You said, 'Don't concern yourself with *us*,' not me. More serious than you want anyone but me to know about. Don't worry, my lips are sealed."

Ria quickly looked back at Vickie and said, "Shush!" then left the room, hunting for the missing mothers.

A moment later, three women came in – Gloria following Ria, Grace right beside her. "Oh, here you are!" Gloria said. "We were looking all over the place for you. I still think we should have had the wedding at the Club. At least, I wouldn't have gotten lost." She fanned herself with the paper announcement. "I'm sorry, dear. Danged hot flashes make me moody. This is your day. Really, if this is where you want to have your wedding, it's fine with us. All of us."

"I hope so since it's almost time. Grace, would you help me with this makeup? I can't get this eyeliner straight and I know Mom can't see up close."

"Oh, I feel so inadequate," Gloria moaned.

"Why don't you help me with my hair?" Ria asked. "I can't see the back of my head and want to make sure I don't have a flat spot. Can you do that for me?"

"Oh, yes, dear. I'm so glad you and Chuck could come. Where is he?"

"I think he met a new old friend. They're getting reacquainted," Ria said.

"Man, I wish he'd get a boyfriend," Grace said. "He's been alone for way too long."

"A boyfriend?" Gloria gasped. "He's gay?"

"Well, duh!" Ria said. "Do you think Dusty would let a straight man hug on Grace like that?"

"Well, I don't know…" Gloria bent back to picking up the curls in Ria's hair and pinning them in place. "I guess it doesn't make any difference," she said.

"I know he goes on dates occasionally, claiming he's 'going out with the guys.' But I've seen the way some men check him out. Women, too, but he never returns their looks. He is the epitome of discretion. I don't think he knows that I know. I tried to bring it up once and he got so flustered and embarrassed, I decided that it really wasn't any of my business. As soon as I'm ready to go out on my own, he can do his own thing, find his Mr. Right, or at least look around for him."

"Wow! That's pretty sensitive," Grace said, sitting back in the chair, overwhelmed with emotions.

"Brought up by a gay dad who is also a non-profit physician," Ria said. "Of course, I'm sensitive! Okay, are we about done here? I'm not wearing any makeup because as the sensitive person that I am, I'll be crying before Vickie takes her first step down the aisle. *Sniff, sniff.* See what I mean?"

Gloria opened her purse and handed Ria an embroidered handkerchief. "Here you go, honey. You can keep it. I packed at least a dozen of them."

"That's a good thing," Grace said, plucking one of them out of her friend's Coach bag, using it to dab under her nose. "I'm glad you planned ahead."

Ria only paid half attention to the banter that was going on as the ladies primped and finalized makeup and hair. "Where's my dad?" she whispered to Grace.

"He dashed out of here before we came to see you. He said he had to go get Vickie's present. What did he get her?"

"Danged if I know. He's back to being Mr. Mysterious again."

***

Chuck sneaked into the back of the wedding hall with his three guests. "Go ahead and sit here in the last row. If anyone asks, you were invited by the family of the bride. The Thornwhistles don't know you're coming, though. Just act like you belong, because you do!" he said, patting the insecure Leanne on her shoulder.

He turned around and saw that Tori had disappeared again. "She won't go far, will she?" he asked Leanne.

"No, she's bashful but not a runner." She looked over at the cluttered coat rack and saw movement. "Two to one she's in there. Don't worry. She didn't want to come but can't go anywhere without us. She may be eighteen, but she doesn't know how to drive on anything other than farm roads."

"Shush!" Luther hissed. "Dang! It's over. That's about the quickest wedding I've ever been to."

"It's the only wedding – other than our own – you've ever been to," Leanne said. "Now come on. I want to meet the bride and groom…and that beautiful young bridesmaid!"

The newlywed couple walked down the aisle in reverse, following the strewn rose petals to the reception hall. Luther, Leanne, and Chuck stepped back, marveling at the beautiful women, waiting until the happy couple and their families had passed before following.

"Grab your daughter, Luther," Leanne said. "She won't come otherwise."

Luther reached into the coats and jackets, his experienced grasp finding her upper arm. "Come on, sweetheart. No one here's going to bite you."

"Can we go home now?" Tori whispered.

125

"There's nothing but rain and gloom in out there now. If you come out willing and behave, I promise you a surprise like nothing you've ever seen or expected."

"Well, she may have seen," Leanne said, "but she certainly isn't expecting this. At least, in this format."

"What are you two babbling about?" Tori asked, her curiosity piqued. "You know I can't resist a mystery."

"Ah, you're right there. Come on. And take off that silly hat!"

Tori pulled off her knit cap, her blonde hair flying everywhere with static electricity. She pushed the blond strands behind her ears and stuck out her chin. "Now, show me something I didn't expect," she said. "Because you know I have a pretty vivid imagination."

Luther held out his arm, waiting for her to join him. "This way, darling. I have a few people I'd like you to meet."

Tori followed, her head down so she didn't have to face the crowd. She was more comfortable with plants and animals than people, and her parents knew it. They were right, though. Western Oregon was nothing but rain and gloom in January. It had started in September and probably wouldn't end until May. It was great for plants but bad for people's humor. She wasn't too fond of knitting and crocheting but spent a lot of time doing both. It was an excuse to keep her head down and away from interacting with people. She sucked it up, curious again about the mystery of seeing something familiar in a new way. A grin grew at the adventure. It couldn't be, could it?

Tori looked around the room, her smile of anticipation as warm and bright as the mood of the people. It was a wedding. She loved weddings. At least, reading about them. This was the first one she'd ever been to. Or almost been to. She grunted with disgust at herself, her shyness stealing her joy again. When would she ever outgrow it? 'One of these days' her parents always said. Well, she'd just have to choose a day. And today – with all these positive vibes, happy voices, and joyous music, the smell of fragrant food and warmth of bodies moving around – this was a good day to claim moodiness was dead. Long live joy and hope.

Clink! Clink! Clink!

All eyes went to the noise of a knife hitting the side of a crystal glass. "Here's to Mr. and Mrs. Richard Rickman," the father of the bride announced. "Health and happiness – and a bit of prosperity – to our very own Rich and Vickie Rickman!"

Tori's eyes widened as she looked at the bride and groom. They had been at the front of the hall when she came in, but their backs were to them. Then she watched as a young woman went up to the bride and gave her a big hug. It looked like the bride was hugging the bride! This version was wearing jeans and flannel, though, just like she was. And she looked just like her except her hair was piled on top of her head in curls instead of down on her shoulders. They were identical twins! Or two of triplets. Both of them looked just like her!

"Mama? What's going on?" Tori asked, her face pale.

"Is this a surprise or what?"

"Do I have sisters you didn't tell me about?"

"Well, yes. Sort of…"

"Papa, did you know about this?"

"Yes, well, sort of…"

Tori glared at them then walked away, right up to the front where the two sisters were still standing close to each other, holding one another's hands.

"Hi," Tori said, her hand thrust out between the two. "I think I'm your sister, Tori. I mean, I'm Tori, and I think I'm your sister."

"Tori!" Ria and Vickie exclaimed, reaching out as two halves of a Siamese twin to grab her close. "We heard there was a third but didn't know where to find you or even your last name. How did you know where to find us?"

Chuck stepped up to the stunned trio. "Vickie, this is your wedding gift: meeting your other sister. Well, I guess it's an engagement gift to you, Ria, and just a surprise to you, Tori."

"But why did you wait so long?" Vickie asked.

"I couldn't do or say anything without permission from Luther and Leanne." Chuck held his hand above his eyebrows and scanned the room, finally finding the elderly couple who had reared Tori as their own, pretending she was their biological daughter. He waved them up. "It took a long time to find them. We thought they were still on the east coast. I think Silas found about two thousand places they *weren't* before starting on the west coast."

"Oregon," Tori said simply. "Eventually." She turned to her sisters. "So, I'm not crazy, right?"

"Why would you think that?" Ria asked.

"Because, well, you know how you can look in the mirror and see your other self? Didn't it ever seem weird, like you should be able to just reach in and grab that other person and pull her out to stand beside you instead of in front of you?"

"Well, kinda," Vickie said, "but I thought everyone felt like that."

"Maybe they do, but I felt something was still missing. Then we moved into a place that had a double mirror in the bathroom. I could move it just so, and then there'd be three of me: me and the two images. It felt so right. I used to get in trouble because I'd take so long in the bathroom. I'd be in there, carrying on conversations in a low voice so no one else would hear. Or rather, my parents wouldn't.

"I always wondered if Mama and Papa were my real parents, too, because I didn't look like either one of them. Plus, they were a little old. Mama even showed me a picture Papa had taken of her nursing me. I'm not quite sure how that was possible, but since Papa can make hair grow on a turnip with the right herbal concoction, then I guess he could have put something together so Mama could get milk."

Tori hooked an arm into each sister's, glad all over again that she wasn't crazy, that there really were two on this earthly plane who looked like her. "So, yes or no: are our biological parents here?"

128

"Yes," Ria and Vickie answered, then looked at each other with raised eyebrows. *Tori looks like us, but she sure is different!*

Tori scanned the room and spotted Grace and Dusty, staring at them, misty-eyed, hugging each other. She nodded to them, acknowledging them. "That was a no-brainer," Tori whispered to her sisters. "Even if we didn't look like them, the reaction on their faces proves it. So, I guess I'll hear the whole story about why they gave us up later. Let me see if I can pick out a grandma or grandpa…"

"We don't have a grandma here," Vickie said. "She's sorta *persona non grata* and also out of the country."

"Fair enough. Everyone has a skeleton or two in the closet. Best to leave them alone, I say." Tori kept looking, bypassing the one older gentleman who looked as interested as her biological parents, but not alike physically. She spotted Silas and noticed his ears, broad shoulders and regal stance. "Him!" she said with complete confidence.

"Nope," Vickie said. "Him," and pointed to Hal. "He's our mother Grace's dad. It's kind of hard not to notice Grace is our mother. She's almost like an older triplet. Or would that be quadruplet?"

Tori shook off the discussion on the mother. "Nope. I'll bet three DNA tests to a donut that he," she said, this time pointing right to Silas, "is Grace's biological father. The other guy definitely has an emotional investment in all of us, but *he's* her father and our grandfather."

Silas watched as the latest triplet to come into his life pointed at him as she carried on an intense conversation with her sisters. Thirty-seven years after Victoria had gotten him drunk and had her way with him, he'd been busted. He looked over the room, pretending to scout out the crowd in general but really looking at Hal's expression. He was looking right at him, crestfallen. He knew.

Hal walked over to him. "I always wondered if I was her bio-dad," Hal said. "It was rumored that Victoria was sowing her last wild oats the week before the wedding, but I always hoped it was just a rumor she started so I'd think she was in demand by others. I didn't want to believe there was any chance another man was Grace's father. It's kind of hard to ignore the family resemblance between you two, but I convinced myself that you were either some long, lost cousin or her ears were a result of a recessive gene popping in. Well, if it was to be anyone, I'm glad it was you."

"Did you ever wonder why I never have more than one drink?" Silas asked.

"And did you ever wonder why I did?" Hal asked, answering his question with his own.

"Do you forgive me?" Silas asked.

"For what? Getting tricked by Victoria? Shit! I'm jealous. You got off easy. I had to live with the bitch for nearly nineteen years!"

Silas tried to hold back his laugh, then saw that Hal was giving into his, so joined him. "We weren't the only two. It's not my place to name names, but she was pretty loose there for a week or two. But you're right. It had to be me. I never realized it, though, until Grace came into the Armstrong family. When she showed up with Victoria, crashing Papa Doc's party, I knew she had to be my issue. Actually, when she started dating Alex, I was glad she was mine."

"So, Papa Doc really was one of the others, then?" Hal asked, tight-lipped.

Silas shrugged his shoulder. "Yes, we both had a butt-pucker moment when we saw Grace and Alex hanging all over each other. We didn't want half-siblings getting carried away. We never said anything directly to each other, but when I saw Papa Doc do a double-take, looking at her ears and then mine, I knew he knew. It was kind of funny, both of us exhaling at the same moment as realization hit." Silas noticed Hal was still grim-faced.

"You are and always have been Grace's daddy. I'm just happy to be one of the guest grandpas to the girls. And now there's one more. By the looks she was giving me, she figured it out within two minutes of being here."

130

"Well, she is your granddaughter. It looks like she got more than the ears from you. She's pretty damned perceptive."

Silas sighed then grinned. "Never a daddy, but now an acknowledged granddaddy. I'm sure glad no one in this family gives two flips about whose blood flows through who."

"Back at ya," Hal said.

Chapter 9: Grand Reception

January 30, 6:00 PM, on the highway

Evan pulled into the gas station to fill up. He checked his phone for messages. *Go ahead and stay a couple more days. I got you covered. Bob*

"What the hell? You couldn't have let me know earlier?" Evan looked at the clock on the dash. Six o'clock. There was no way he'd make it back in time for the wedding, but he could be there for the reception. And maybe more one-on-one time with Ria and her 'I can't get pregnant this way' solution to his pre-wedding excitement. He shifted in the seat, not wanting to remember their stolen half-hour together before he got out to fuel the van.

Stepping into the cold blast of late January pre-blizzard took care of any residual stiffness. "Just grab a couple of granola bars and the biggest cup of coffee that will fit in the cupholder, and then it's back to Massachusetts."

Evan picked through the snack section, finding the meal bars with the least amount of sugar, then waited for the man in the kilt to finish filling his coffee mug. "Nice cup," he said to the man.

"Thank you. My son made this." The Scot held up the artisan cup with 'Da' inscribed in the side. "He's quite the artisan."

"He certainly is," Evan said, reaching up to touch the colorful glaze. He turned to the counter, unable to look away from the confrontation. "Looks like someone is having a bad day."

"Aye, that's my wife givin' the owner a fit. We had a flat tire and no spare. He's sayin' we'll have to wait a day or two fer another to get here. She's unwillin' to wait and insists he take one from his own vehicle and sell it to us so we can be on our way." The man took a pocket watch out of his sporran and checked the time. "I think we already missed the weddin' but if we were able to get out of here now, we'd be able to get to the reception."

"Strange. That's my story, too, except for the flat tire part,"

Evan said. "You wouldn't be going to Vickie and Rich Rickman's wedding, would you?"

"Aye! We would! Are you sayin' that's where yer headin'?"

"Aye, I mean, yes! As soon as I pay for the gas I just bought and this, I'm heading that way. I have room for you in my van. You and your wife are welcome to join me."

"I hope it's a big van. I have a few bairns to bring along, too."

"I may not have enough seatbelts for everyone, but unless you have a dozen in your tribe, we'll make it."

"Ach, I only have seven plus the one in the oven. Come on. Let's tell her the great news."

"Excuse me, Wife," Angus said. "I have a solution to our dilemma. Sir," Angus said, addressing the frazzled store owner, "is it all right with you if we leave our vehicle here fer a bit? I've acquired a ride to our destination. Go ahead, if you don't mind, and order the tire fer us. We'll be back to pay fer yer time and trouble after the celebration."

The harried man looked from the big Scot to Evan and back again. Seeing the grins on both faces, he felt it grow on his own. "Anything to keep her from asking me again," he said.

Evan handed him a hundred-dollar bill. "This is for the gas, coffee, and these snacks." He put up his hand, asking him to wait, then hustled back to the meal bars, grabbing ten more. "And these. If there's anything left, apply it to their bill. Come on, folks. We have a wedding reception to attend!"

By the time Evan had the windows washed and mirrors readjusted, the tribe of Scots had piled in and settled on the bed, captain's chair, or floor with a minimum of discussion and no arguments. "You have a well-behaved family... I'm sorry," Evan said, as he settled into his seat and buckled up. "We never exchanged names. I'm Evan Fraser."

"Ach, another Scot! I'm Angus McDermott. The name's Irish for that was my grandsire's name, but we're Scots."

"Or have taken up with them. Just call me 'Ma," Friday said.

"I'd tell you the name of all our sons, but since you can't see their faces yet, it wouldn't make a difference. I just holler, 'Son,' and they all come running."

"Are you friends or family of the bride or groom?" Evan asked.

"We were invited by a friend of the bride," Friday answered, then looked back at her husband, scowling. *Let me do the talking, please.*

"What she said," Angus echoed. "I'm jest here as the backup sitter fer the bairns."

Evan looked over at Ma's swollen belly. "Is it time for a daughter?"

"After having seven sons in thirteen years, I certainly hope so!"

"Now, dinna I tell you I'd give you all the bairns you'd want? I never said anythin' about whether they'd be sons or daughters. That's up to the Almighty, not me."

Evan took a snack bar out of the sack, then handed the plastic bag to Ma. "Take one, then send the rest back. I don't know when you ate last, but it's been a long day for me. We have at least another hour and a half. That is, if I drive the speed limit."

"Don't hold back on our account," Friday said, then used her teeth to rip the corner of the plastic wrapper. "Speed limits are for those who don't have a deadline." She took a big bite of the nut and grain concoction and chewed the first food she had eaten in the last thirteen years that wasn't prepared by her. She bent over and used the glow of the dash lights to read the ingredients. Half of them she'd never heard of, all with -ite or -ose at the end. Garbage chemicals. She gulped the mass down, then handed the rest of the snack bar back to her husband. "Let the boys share these. I'm not as hungry as I thought."

Evan's mind was awhirl, concentrating on his speed – keeping it nine miles over the limit – calculating his rate in miles per hour and the distance to the wedding venue, trying to estimate their time of arrival.

Friday was anxious to find out who this generous young man

was but leery of engaging him in conversation. She had stayed off everyone's radar for years and it was only curiosity that brought her out today. Chuck had told her via Silas that it was Vickie's wedding. So, if Chuck had a relationship with Vickie, was it be possible that Ria knew she had another sister? She shook her head, trying to stifle the question she'd asked herself dozens of times a day since she'd first got the invitation. And what about the third one? Tori Lynn, the one who was adopted by that aging hippie couple? Had they stayed connected with Vickie's family?

"If you don't mind, I'm going to take a nap," she said to Evan. Emotionally, she was exhausted. Being eight months pregnant had also zapped a great deal of her energy. She sighed, happy to have a homecoming of sorts, but also glad she had made the decision to stay with Angus. Legally, they weren't married, but that was only because she wasn't ready to share her legal name with anyone, bring herself back into the real world or onto any agency's database. It didn't matter. As far as she was concerned, she was Mrs. Angus McDermott or Ma, forever and ever. Amen!

"We're here, Ma," Evan said, gently touching her shoulder. "We made good time. We're only fifteen minutes late."

"Huh? Oh, yeah. Just in time to make a grand entrance, I'm sure. Come on, sons. Let's find a bathroom and clean up a bit first."

Angus carried his youngest son over his shoulder, the other ones holding each other's hands in pairs as they followed behind him. "I got this," Angus said. "Jest go see to yer own needs."

"This way," Evan said, leading the way to the back entrance. The bathrooms are to your left."

Evan left the Scots and headed to the noisy banquet hall. Endless chatter and clanking plates and glasses verified the ceremony was over and the dinner and toasting had begun. He looked up at the long table in front of the hall and gasped. "Three? There really is another one?"

The three identical women – two dressed in flannel and denim, the other the bride in white – were in an intense discussion. He

135

couldn't be certain, but one of the flannel-clad ladies looked a little bit different. Ah, that's what it was. Her hair was wild. Ria wouldn't attend her sister's wedding with hair that looked like it had been kept under a knit cap for the last two years! Yes, his Ria was perfectly coifed with curls piled atop her head. He looked at two of the other women dressed in flannel. Only Ms. Wild Hair was wearing blue, a brilliant azure plaid that accentuated the color of her eyes. And those of her sisters, too.

They had to be triplets! There was no other explanation.

"Amazing, right?" Ma asked.

"Did you know there were three of them?" Evan asked.

"Yup, but I haven't seen the other two since they were a couple of hours old."

"Which other two? I mean, which sister are you here for?"

"Ria."

"Hey! Are you Friday?" Evan asked, suddenly remembering the story of Ria's early years.

"How'd you guess."

"I suppose it's your nurturing spirit. Besides, Ria told me you ran off and married a Scot. No denying him. Looks like you two still get along famously."

Friday patted her belly. "Is it that obvious?"

"Let's wait for a break in their conversation. May I present you? Oh, and you know I'm Evan Fraser, but what you don't know is that I'm Ria's fiancé."

"Hmm. I always knew that girl made wise choices. Oh, lookie there…" Friday nodded to Chuck. "My old bed mate."

"But I thought he was gay," Evan whispered.

"He is. I didn't say we ever had sex. Did you see that little RV we lived in? It was not much bigger than your van."

"Actually, I did. For about a minute. I was with Silas when we delivered their new one. Or their gently used one. Ria said it was the first time she'd had her own room. By the way, she's an RN now. Got her degree and is working on getting further certification. She may not be the youngest certified nurse in the state, but by the time she takes her finals, she may be the youngest Advanced Nurse Practioner on the east coast."

"Good for her. Hey, look. I think now's our chance." Friday looked back at Angus and the boys and waved. "Give me a moment, and then I'll introduce you."

"Go aheid. We'll await yer signal," Angus said, bouncing the two-year-old toddler on his shoulder.

"Congratulations, Vickie, Rich," Evan said, his hand out to shake Rich's. "I get to kiss the bride, right?" he asked the groom.

"Just don't get carried away," Rich said.

"Or start comparing us," Ria said, laughing.

Evan gave Vickie a gentle kiss on the cheek. "I'm sorry I missed the wedding. I was halfway back to school and got a text from my roommate, telling me he'd cover my shifts for the next forty-eight hours. I figured I could at least come and toast to your good health and happiness."

"Well, being married assures the second one, but not necessarily the first, so I appreciate the blessings," Vickie said. "Who's your friend?" she asked, noticing the stares and sly smile on the pregnant woman he'd brought with him.

"Oh, her?" Evan said, grinning. "Just someone who came along for the ride. Actually, you haven't seen Vickie in how long?" he asked Friday.

"Eighteen years and twenty-seven days," she answered.

"Friday?" Ria asked, then shouted, "Friday! It's you! Oh, my God! You're huge! I guess you and Angus are still together. Oh, my God! I knew I'd recognize you if I ever saw you again. I mean, you look a lot different being pregnant and all..." Ria paused to take a breath and try to rein in her babbling, then burst out crying.

"I've missed you," she wept, hugging her surrogate mother.

"I've missed you, too," Friday said, crying just as much.

"Here," Gloria said, coming up to hand both of them a handkerchief. "I brought lots of them."

"Who's she?" Vickie whispered to Chuck.

"She's the woman who helped me smuggle you and your sisters away from the crook who told Grace you were dead."

"She what?" Vickie screeched.

"Hey, long story that I thought you knew. I'll tell you all about it someday. But not today. Just know that she's a great person, so be nice."

"So, is she one of my presents, too?" Vickie asked.

"Nah, you're one of hers. I knew she's wanted to see all three of you again. As far as I know, this is the first time all three of you have been together since the day you were born. Meeting Tori is a present to both you and Ria."

Ria moved over to Chuck, pulling on Friday's hand to join them. "Dad, are you responsible for Friday coming tonight?"

"Guilty," he said. "Oh, and I think you remember Angus." Chuck turned around and motioned for the big man surrounded by young males of stair-stepping sizes to join him.

"Oh, my God! Are all these your sons, Friday?" Ria asked.

"Hers and mine," Angus answered.

"Why does she call you Friday, Ma?" the red-haired boy who looked to be four years old asked.

"Because before I was Ma, I was called Friday. But you still call me Ma, all right?"

"Yes, Ma," he said, then sniggered into his hands.

"These are my sons," Friday said, her face beaming with pride. She began at the oldest and started naming them. "This is Young Angus, Brian, the twins Colum and Dougal, Ethan, Fergus, and Gavin. We're hoping this one is our Hannah, but we'll have to wait about six or seven weeks to find out if she sneaked in or we're getting a Hamish or Hector."

"You never had a daughter?" Vickie asked.

Friday skirted the answer by saying, "Ria is the only daughter I ever brought up, and that was for a little less than five years. It seems that Chuck did a fine job by himself." She looked over at

138

Chuck, now standing close to Evan's father, their hands at their sides, barely touching. "Or did he find someone?"

"Not that I know of, but I'm not privy to his private life," Vickie said, a sly smirk arising. The two men were discreet, but anyone who saw the two men in the same room couldn't help but see their longing gazes and coy smiles.

Vickie stood on her tiptoes and looked over the crowd. "I don't know how many people my parents invited. I swear I don't know half of them."

"Almost half of them are *my* family," Friday joked, then looked over the crowd. Standing next to the bride, she felt amazingly comfortable in the presence of someone she'd just met. Suddenly, she reached out and grabbed Vickie's hand. "Who's that woman?" she asked.

"I don't know. Mom, Ria, do you know who she is?" Vickie asked.

"No, dear," Gloria answered. "She must be one of the dozen 'extras' Chuck asked me to make accommodations for. I'm pretty sure I've never seen her before."

"Ditto," Ria said. "She kind of looks familiar, though."

Chuck had been eavesdropping, his all-knowing smile wide.

Ria and Friday both noticed it and looked to each other as they had in the past, their silent agreement acknowledged. "Go for it," Ria said.

Friday opened her mouth to ask, then looked again at the woman. She was smiling at her. A loving smile that brought tears to Friday's eyes.

"Is she?" she asked Chuck.

"Yup. Took Silas nearly fifteen years to find her…" he began.

Friday didn't wait for the rest of his answer. She 'excuse me'd' through the standing and seated crowd to the young woman she recognized as her daughter.

"It's you! It's really you, isn't it?" Friday asked, tears streaming down her face.

"Yes, I'm pretty sure," the woman answered, her tears just as numerous. "I mean, we can do another DNA test, but according to Mr. Silas, it's a sure thing." Not waiting for an invitation, she reached around and did her best to hug her very pregnant mother.

"Sorry," she said. "It looks like we're both expecting. This is my first. Are those my brothers over there?"

"Seven brothers," Friday said, then patted her belly. "We don't know about this one yet. She's not due for another six weeks."

"She? Does this mean you're claiming a daughter?"

"The only daughter I'm claiming is you. Did you have a good life? I mean, did you get loving parents and a decent place to live?"

The woman nodded, then turned to an empty place setting on the table beside her and took a cloth napkin to wipe her nose. "Excuse me," she said.

"I'm sorry," Friday said. "I don't even know your new name."

"Rhianna. My parents said it was written on the label of the little gown I was wearing when they got me. They liked it, so it stayed. Is that the name you gave me?"

"Yes, it is." Friday felt a hand on her shoulder and turned aside.

"For your daughter," Gloria said, her eyes red-rimmed from crying. "Congratulations!"

Clink! Clink! Clink!

Roger waited for everyone to stop talking. "As the father of the bride, I'd like to thank all of you for coming. I see we have a few surprise guests tonight, too. It looks more like a family reunion than a wedding, but the bottom line is, we're family. Whether we were born into a family, legally adopted, or 'claimed,' I think everyone here is connected one way or another to each other. Here's to family!" he said, raising his champagne flute in toast. "Forever may we remember and love one another!"

"Here! Here!" and cheers answered his toast.

"Now, Chuck, you seem to be the instigator of about half of these reunions..."

"Or maybe all of them..." Chuck said with a sly smile.

"So, are there any more surprises you'd like to share?"

Chuck looked at Keith and grinned. "Well, I guess one more to share with family won't break the scales. Ladies and gentlemen, I'd like to introduce my fiancé, Keith Fraser."

Evan's father eased himself out of his chair, red-faced and chagrined. "I guess there's no better way for Chuck to come out than among friends. For those of you who don't know, I was widowed a few years back. I didn't think anyone could fill that void, but Chuck did. We've known each other since college, but with one thing or another – including children for both of us and my marriage to John – we drifted apart. We'll wait for our children to be married first, but in the meantime, here's to love and family, and happy ever afters!"

"Mama, what's he talking about, marrying another man," Tori asked.

"Hush," Leanne said. "I'll let your father explain it to you later."

Tori looked over at her newly discovered sisters. Their faces were bright with happiness, clapping, whistling and cheering for Chuck and Keith and their announcement. "I guess that's another part of the world that's been kept from me for eighteen years. Looks like I have a lot of living to catch up on."

The End

Afterword

Would you like to know more about Chuck, Grace and Dusty, and all those wannabe grandpas? I intentionally went back in time to late 1991 and early 1992 to begin this saga. Here's a quick overview of the upcoming stories:

Grace – Surviving an evil mother was just the first of her challenges. A gritty women's fiction story. *The Set Up*

Vickie – Gloria and Roger's daughter – is dealing with lifestyles of the rich and famous – and devious – in *Diamonds Aren't for Everyone*

Ria – Brought up in the backwoods by a single father dedicated to helping those less fortunate, she also has *That Magic Touch.* Is there more to life than healing and living on the edge? Would Evan be the one to show her what made life bright and enjoyable?

Tori – An independent free thinker brought up by hippie parents who grow wine grapes and pot, Tori tries not to fall in love with the new hand with the sexy voice in *How Love Grows.*

Silas – Everyone's friend, confidant, and go-to guy in this series, has his own story. The young woman he met at Woodstock in 1969 has shown up in his life again. Will they make a go of it? Will her secret ruin their possibility of a second-chance romance? Find out more about him in *They Call Me Sherlock.*

Thanks for reading, and remember, authors love to get honest reviews!

About the Author

 Author Dani Haviland started writing late in life and has been making up for lost time with a flood of works from sports, rom-coms, historicals, time travel, and Sweet and Sassy romances to Unforgettable romantic suspense and cozy mystery tales – with a few short stories thrown in to round out the reading experience.

Dani is also the owner of Chill Out! Books, one of the publishers for The Authors' Billboard. Follow her on Amazon and BookBub to make sure you get her latest stories.

Contact information:

Website: www.danihaviland.com

Facebook: Dani Haviland Author and Dani Haviland & Friends

Readers Group: http://bit.ly/2DaniStTeam

BookBub: http://bit.ly/BBDani

Goodreads: http://bit.ly/2DHgdrds

Email: dani@danihaviland.com

Twitter: @dani_haviland and @gr8authors

I love to hear from readers!

Sign up for my newsletter to get the latest information on new releases, free stuff, and contests at: http://bit.ly/2DHnews

Other Books by Dani Haviland

ARLIE UNDERCOVER SERIES

(romantic suspense based in Alaska and Arizona)

A Stingray Christmas: (Book One) Anchorage detective on medical leave travels from Alaska to Arizona to see for the first time the son he'd fathered as an anonymous sperm donor. Great and rotten surprises await the cop with the smartest smartphone around.

The Biggest Heart Ever: (Book Two) When would Arlie learn that trying to do everything by himself could be deadly—and make Charlene a widow before they were married?

Always a Bigger Fish: (Book Three) Back in Alaska, Arlie finds out he's a target. Will vacationing detective Billy Burke (from THE FAIRIES SAGA) have information to help nab the scalper?

How to Fix a Broken Life: (Book Four) When Arlie's very pregnant wife is kidnapped by pseudo terrorists, will he be the one to rescue her or will a surprise hero come in to save the day?

Because You Said So: (Book Five) Something's amiss at the Port of Anchorage. Will Arlie be able to solve it and still be back in time to wear the Santa suit?

Heaven and Heartbreak: (Book Six) How will Louie handle being a daddy? And what about that baby momma?

TRIPLETS: THREE AREN'T ONE

The Set Up: (Book One) Grace's story. How it all began with the mother from hell.

Diamonds Aren't for Everyone: (Book Two) Vickie's story – Growing up a billionaire.

That Magic Touch: (Book Three) Ria's story – Doctoring in the backwoods with secrets.

How Love Grows: (Book Four) Tori's story – Growing up in vineyards and marijuana farms.

They Call Me Sherlock: (Book Five) – Back to Woodstock with a friend.

THE FAIRIES SAGA SERIES
(historical fiction/time travel, listed in order):

Kibbles and Bits: FREE ebook: Sample the first stories in the series before you buy. The Fairies Saga stories. Find out how the first five books got their crazy names, too.

Naked in the Winter Wind: (Book One) How does an older woman wind up as a young hottie in Revolutionary War era North Carolina? First book in the time travel series.

Ha'Penny Jenny: (Book Two) More about the naïve and psychic young girl who was adopted into a time traveling family. Will her past catch up to her?

Aye, I am a Fairy: (Book Three) Young British lord finds himself entwined with a time traveling family and must decide if he should go back in time, too.

Dances Naked: (Book Four) Directionally challenged time traveler is rescued by Cherokee in 18th century. What must he do before the chief will show him to The Trees, the portal through time?

Chasing Christmas: (Book Five) A young Cherokee is rescued from an abusive man and changes the lives of many in this 18th century America family.

The Great Big Fairy: (Book Six) Very tall Benji grew up in the 20th century but was born in the 18th. When he finds a way to return to his grandparents in the distant past, he goes for it. Once there, he realizes he can't stay, but must return to the future.

Little Bear and the Ladies: (Book Seven) What's a bachelor trapper to do with all the females he rescues from the Hessian mercenaries? He'd better hurry and figure something!

Little Drummer Boy: (Book Eight) Young Scout works to earn money for a home in post-Revolutionary War America but runs up against prejudices and snowstorms.

Never Too Young: (Book Nine) Scout and Ha'Penny Jenny have grown up, but will they be able to spend their life together, or will the past and ruffians get in their way?

Time in a Little Blue Bottle: (Book Ten) Elvis, Mark Twain, and the prime vampire are racing to get the bottle of Fountain of Youth water before sweet Bella and the youthful pickpocket. So why are time travelers Marty Melbourne and Master Simon interested?

Kidnapped!: (Book Eleven) Benji's sister has been abducted and he and his Scottish police officer brother-in-law will do anything to get her back...even trust the mysterious letter sent by an ancestor, a convict on The First Fleet into Australia!

Big Mac: (Book Twelve) Can Big Mac stop his sire, the errant Viking time traveler, from starting a pandemic?

BENJI, THE LOST YEARS
(contemporary novellas about a young Benji MacKay)

Pool Boy Wanted: No Experience Preferred: (rather racy) Young Benji has been a hostage and slave, but life gets worse when an older woman decides she wants him as her own.

Luke the Unexpected: Love of classic motorcycles brought them together, but Luke and Holly have other challenges to face. Find out how their friend Benji got his stripes here.

STAND ALONE NOVELLAS
(contemporary romances)

Kit Kringle: An Alaskan Tale: Kay moved to Alaska for the wrong reasons, then decided to stay and start her own business. What she hadn't planned on were prejudices and falling in love.

Be My Angel: Wyatt's dream to help save the wild mustangs began with the purchase of a rundown ranch in western Oregon. What he hadn't anticipated was being mesmerized by a sassy woman in a wheelchair.

Three Are One: The post chaplain tried to help the young widow adjust, but would his feelings for her and the search for his lost sister cause problems?

One Arctic Summer: That unforgettable summer of 1994 in Barrow, Alaska, and the touch she never forgot...If she goes back, will he remember her?

The Polar Xpress: Will the California chiropractor get a first chance at romance with the owner of Second Chance Kennels when he is stranded in Alaska?

Too Fast For You: Ten years after Little League, two talented professional baseball players wind up on the same minor league team. Will she remember him? And will their friendship be ruined if she does?

www.ingramcontent.com/pod-product-compliance
Lightning Source LLC
Chambersburg PA
CBHW061244170626
46809CB00007B/2816